W9-AUD-702

LILY AND THE LAWMAN

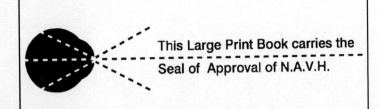

This Large Print Book carries the Seal of Approval of N.A.V.H.

LILY AND THE LAWMAN

ERICA VETSCH

THORNDIKE PRESS

A part of Gale, Cengage Learning

GALE
CENGAGE Learning

Detroit • New York • San Francisco • New Haven, Conn • Waterville, Maine • London

GALE
CENGAGE Learning™

Copyright © 2010 by Erica Vetsch.
Idaho Brides Series #2.
All scripture quotations are taken from the King James Version of the Bible.
Thorndike Press, a part of Gale, Cengage Learning.

Thorndike Press® Large Print Christian Historical Fiction.
The text of this Large Print edition is unabridged.
Other aspects of the book may vary from the original edition.
Set in 16 pt. Plantin.

LIBRARY OF CONGRESS CATALOGING-IN-PUBLICATION DATA

Vetsch, Erica.
   Lily and the lawman / by Erica Vetsch. — Large print ed.
     p. cm. — (Idaho brides series; #2.) (Thorndike Press large print Christian historical fiction)
   ISBN-13: 978-1-4104-4002-0 (hardcover)
   ISBN-10: 1-4104-4002-8 (hardcover)
   1. Large type books. I. Title.
PS3622.E886L55 2011
813'.6—dc22   2011017753

Published in 2011 by arrangement with Barbour Publishing, Inc.

Printed in Mexico
1 2 3 4 5 6 7 15 14 13 12 11

To Linda Ambrose.
Thank you for everything.

ONE

Money Creek, Idaho Territory, 1883

No man should have to arrest his own father — at least not more than once a month.

"Where is he this time?" Trace McConnell stopped polishing his rifle stock and let his booted feet fall off the corner of the desk to the floor of the sheriff's office. Resignation crept over him like the shadow of a cloud moving across the hills.

"The Golden Slipper. You'd better get down there. He's causing quite a ruckus. Griffith took after him with a broom." The town barber hooked his thumbs in his white apron ties.

Trace stood. He smoothed his mustache and glanced down at the badge on his shirt. A tiny thrust of pride shot through him. An honest-to-goodness lawman at last — even if it might be temporary.

The shouting had barely died down from the town meeting. He'd never expected to be appointed, what with his past history and all, but Colonel Bainbridge and the parson had overridden the naysayers, and the job was his until Sheriff Powers healed up from his accident. Some had felt that as a former prisoner in the town jail, he was unqualified to be the acting sheriff, but in the end, the colonel had his way.

"What's he done now?"

"The usual. Wants a bottle when he's skinfull already."

Trace ducked under the door frame and stepped onto the boardwalk. He settled his hat onto his head and started a slow walk up the block. The morning sun beat down strong, and a dusty breeze blew into his face, promising another hot day. Shouts and clanging metal ricocheted down the street. A horse broke loose from its hitching post and veered toward him at a canter. Trace stood still and let the animal pass.

Albert Powers leaned against a porch post halfway along the main street, a sling encasing his right arm, snow-white in the sunshine.

Trace kept his expression neutral as he drew near the prickly sometime sheriff of Money Creek.

Powers sneered. " 'Bout time you got here, McConnell." The portly man waved his cane up the street. "Get over there and arrest him before he hurts someone."

Trace kept walking.

A group of townsfolk stood in the street, curious and quiet.

A spittoon sailed out of the alley between the saloon and the Rusty Bucket Café and rolled in a wide arc before coming to rest in the middle of the road. Georgia, the café owner, stood in her doorway, a pencil stuck in the knot of frazzled red hair at the back of her head. Miss Whitman stood beside her, a dishcloth dangling from her hand.

Trace swallowed against the humiliation climbing his throat. Though he'd never so much as spoken to Lily Whitman, something about her caught his attention every time he saw her. It was those eyes. He pulled his gaze away.

"Morning, Trace. He's liquored up and snarling like a spring bear. Must've caroused pretty good last night." Georgia crossed her arms over her wide flowered apron. "He's been fighting and cussing something terrible."

Before Trace could enter the alley, a wiry, filthy man staggered out. Iron gray hair hung in his bloodshot eyes. Stubble peppered his sunken cheeks.

The smell smote Trace from ten paces

away — unwashed male, sour whiskey, and spittoon dregs. He grimaced. "Morning, Pa."

The downtrodden Angus McConnell spun on his heel and staggered a couple of paces before righting himself. The top of his left sleeve had ripped away from his jacket, showing the filthy flannel shirt underneath. He squinted then smeared his hand across his mouth. "He won't give me no more whiskey. Make him give me a bottle." He pointed a craggy finger with a broken yellow nail toward the balding man emerging from between the buildings.

Mr. Griffith gripped his broom handle across his body as if to prevent a charge and stepped up onto the Golden Slipper porch. "I told you no more whiskey. You're drunk enough. Go sleep it off, Gus."

Gus lurched and caught himself before he fell. "I ain't near drunk. What kind of saloonkeeper are you, refusing to serve good customers like me?"

Trace stepped in front of his father. "Let's go. You coming peaceful this time?" Trace didn't hold out much hope of that. The eyes of the town bored through him, watching his every move. Shame at his father's condition licked at him like a hundred candle flames.

10

"I ain't going nowhere with you. You want to take me to jail. I've been there, and there ain't no whiskey down at the jail." Gus raised himself up to his full height — a good eight inches shorter than his tallest son.

Trace took a step forward. "You don't need whiskey. You need some sleep. And a bath. When was the last time you had a decent meal?"

"Leave me alone. I don't need your interference. I'm gonna poke that stingy barkeep in the nose. Stay out of my way or I'll pound you, too." He shook his fist up at Trace, swaying.

Trace looked skyward for a moment then shouldered his rifle. He grabbed Gus by his skinny upper arm and turned him toward the jail. "Come along quiet. You've caused enough trouble for one day, and it isn't even nine o'clock."

Gus flailed and cussed, spittle flying. "You can't do this to me. I ain't done nothing. It ain't against the law to have a little drink."

Trace tightened his grip on Gus's arm. "You're disturbing the peace. *Again.* If you don't settle down and come along quiet, I'll have to cuff you." He'd rather not with the whole town watching, but the law was the law, and he'd shackle the prisoner if he had to.

11

Movement to his right caught Trace's eye.

Cal emerged from the telegraph office and walked across the porch in front of the café. He touched his hat brim to Georgia and Miss Whitman and jumped down onto the road. Puffs of dust shot out from under his boots.

Trace nodded at his younger brother.

Cal's face settled into grim lines when he stared hard at Gus.

"Don't give me none of your lip, you jackanapes." Gus glared back. "Don't know what this world's coming to when a man can't even count on his family to back him up. You're all against me — you, Trace, and Alec."

Trace started up the street once more.

Cal fell into step on the other side of Gus, snagging Gus's other arm and force-marching him upright between them.

Trace gave Gus a little shake. "You leave Alec out of this. And Cal, too, for that matter. I'm the law in these parts, and you're disturbing the peace. I have no choice but to arrest you. Family or not doesn't come into it."

"Blood should be thicker than water!" Gus shouted for the whole town to hear.

"Blood should be thicker than whiskey, too, but that never stopped you before. Quit

12

your bellowing and settle down."

Powers waited for them near the jail. His nose wrinkled as they got close. "This time, Gus, the judge should throw away the key. You're a nuisance. McConnell, make sure you clear all the bedding out of his cell. Last time he was sick as a cat all over the bed, and it took a week to get the place aired out." Trace and Cal dragged Gus onto the boardwalk, and as they entered the cramped little jail, Powers kicked Gus in the seat of the pants.

Trace stopped, his hand falling away from his father. He turned to face Powers, anger coiling through him. His grip tightened on his rifle and he forced his voice to stay even. "I'd appreciate it if you'd leave him be."

Powers blinked as if Trace had shouted at him; then he blustered back, "He isn't worth the trouble. Don't you give him any special treatment. Don't know why the town council foisted you on me. I'll be healed up soon, and you'll be out of a job. So don't get too comfortable with that badge. You're only the acting sheriff." He limped away, leaning heavily on his cane.

The cell keys clanked when Trace took them from the desk. Cal clanged the iron-barred door shut behind Gus. Gus tried to bore holes in Trace with his glare when the key scraped in the lock, shutting him in.

"I'll see about getting you a bath and some clean clothes." Trace tossed the keys back in the drawer.

"Don't do me no favors." Gus kicked the metal bucket in the corner of the cell.

"You want something to eat?" Trace knew the answer but asked anyway.

"No, I don't want anything to eat. I want some whiskey!"

Cal snorted then dug in his pocket. "Message came in for you on the stage this morning. I told Shorty I'd bring it to you." He handed Trace a paper.

Trace sagged into the chair behind the desk and scanned the page. "U.S. Marshal is on his way here. Says he got a line on a child kidnapping operation and wants me to go along as an extra gun." A smile tugged at Trace's lips, but he quelled it.

Cal grinned. "If you impress a U.S. Marshal, maybe you'll be hired on permanent. Powers can have his tin-pot sheriff's job back, and you won't have to put up with him anymore."

Gus threw the bucket at the bars. "Lemme outta here, or get me some whiskey!"

Trace raised one eyebrow at Cal. "What, and leave all this?"

■ ■ ■ ■

Lily Whitman pressed her hands to the small of her back and arched away from the stiffness. She tried to smile when Georgia clomped by and clattered another tower of dishes onto the counter by the washtub. Lily swiped with a wet wrist at the tendrils of hair floating across her forehead, sweeping them back before plunging her hands into the hot water. "Is this the last of them?"

Georgia stirred the stew pot with a huge ladle, her apron swaying with her movements. "For now. Noon rush will be on us before we know it."

Stubborn egg and sticky honey clung to the dishes, making Lily's arm ache as she scrubbed. "Seems like there are more customers all the time." Lily missed her sister's helpful hands in the restaurant kitchen.

"You don't have anybody to blame for that but yourself." Georgia leaned against the worktable and wiped her hands on the towel tucked at her waist.

"How's that?" Lily smiled, having learned not to take offense at anything Georgia might say. The woman had a tongue like a bull-hide whip and a heart as soft as whipped cream.

15

"It's your baking. I can cook good, plain food, and I can slap together pies well enough that the customers don't complain, but since you came and started making all those cakes and pastries and biscuits so light they need gravy to keep them from floating right up into the air, the folks in this town line up to get a table." She picked up a cloth and began wiping dishes and stowing them on the shelves in preparation for lunch. "Violet's cough just gets worse and worse. I wish there was something I could do for her."

Lily scrubbed harder. "You've already been too good to us, Georgia. I don't know what we would've done without you."

"Maybe you should run up and check on Violet and Rose before the lunch rush starts. And you can bring the baby back here if she's awake. I'll finish the dishes. It's just Seb Lewis and some of the old-timers sitting in the dining room chewing the fat and soaking up coffee, and I can look after them."

Lily hurried to do Georgia's bidding, sending up a prayer of thanks that God had brought Georgia into the Whitman girls' lives at just the right moment. Not everyone would've hired a woman in Violet's condition, her being unwed and all. Georgia

16

mothered Violet and showered love on the baby. Seeing the giant red-haired woman and the tiny blond baby laughing and cooing at each other always made Lily smile.

The stairs jutting up the outside of the building creaked under Lily's feet as she ascended to the tiny loft over the café. Georgia had given them the room along with jobs and had helped them shove the crates and sacks of restaurant supplies to one side to clear a space for an iron bedstead and washstand. She'd even gotten a friend to nail a couple of pieces of curved wood on the bottom of a crate to make a cradle for Rose. After eight months of working at the Rusty Bucket, Lily realized that most of Georgia's profits were going to pay Lily and Violet's wages. Georgia's generosity made Lily work all the harder to please her boss.

Lily opened the loft door and ducked inside, letting her eyes adjust to the dim light. Rose lay on her back, her chubby hands clutching a string of wooden spools. Pink, round cheeks, bow-shaped lips, and a halo of fair, wispy hair.

"Vi?" Lily skirted boxes of tinned peaches to stand next to the bed.

The lump under the covers didn't move. Concern skittered across Lily's skin. She eased the quilt back from her sister's face.

As Lily placed the back of her hand against Violet's damp forehead, Violet began to shake with a chill. Her eyes opened at Lily's touch, and a spasm of coughs burst from her.

"Oh, Vi, did you take your medicine? Is it not helping?" Lily grimaced with guilt for not checking on her sooner. She turned to the washstand and dampened a cloth. "I'm going to get the doctor."

Violet shook her head. "We can't afford a doctor. We're still paying him for last time."

The weight of responsibility settled more heavily on Lily's shoulders. It seemed they no sooner got a bit ahead than something happened to take their reserves. Rose outgrew her clothes, or Violet needed her medicine bottle refilled, or a hole wore right through the sole of Lily's only pair of shoes. At this rate they'd never have enough put by to open a bakery.

Violet coughed again then lay back, her breath wheezing. A tear slid down her thin cheek. "I'm sorry, Lily."

"Sorry?" Lily sponged her sister's face and neck. "What do you have to be sorry for? You can't help being sick." They'd traveled this road so many times since Violet had fallen ill.

She clutched Lily's arm. "I'm sorry you

have to care for me. I'm sorry for being so foolish about Bobby and for getting in the family way. I'm sorry you're not back home in Boise with Father running the bakery instead of living in this cramped room and slaving in that hot kitchen downstairs." She gasped for air and convulsed with coughs again. "I'm sorry to be such a burden to you."

Lily loosened her wrist from Violet's weak grasp. "I have no regrets, and I don't want you to either. I wouldn't go back to Father for all the bakeries in Boise. When he disowned you, I disowned him. Men are nothing but trouble in this world, and we don't need them. You and I and Rose are just fine on our own."

Rose squawked at the sound of her name and banged the spools on the side of her makeshift crib.

Violet sniffled. "Promise me, Lily. Promise me you'll do whatever it takes to take care of Rose."

Lily sponged Violet's hot face once more. Her sister's demand was a frequent and familiar one, and Lily responded as she always did. "I'll always take care of Rose. I promise."

Two

The U.S. Marshal was nothing like Trace expected. For starters, the man was dog-sick. He flopped off his horse and staggered into the jail. Fever gleamed in his eyes and flushed his cheeks. "You McConnell?" His voice rasped as if it hurt him to speak.

"That's right." Trace stood from behind the desk, taking note of the star pinned on the man's jacket. "Marshal Maxwell?"

The man sneezed and dug in his pocket, pulling out a crumpled red handkerchief. "Barely. Can someone tend to my horse?"

Cal nodded and sauntered toward the door.

Trace went to the stove in the corner and stuffed kindling inside the firebox. "Coffee?" He had intended to take the marshal down to the café, but the man looked as if he might topple over at any moment. "Go on and sit." He motioned to the chair behind the desk.

"Much obliged. Never should've left Boise, but I couldn't afford to wait." He sneezed again and hugged his arms close as if to ward off a chill. "I've been chasing my tail with these missing children, and I've finally got something to go on."

Cal returned with the marshal's saddlebags slung over his broad shoulder. "Figured you might want these." He handed them to the marshal. "Your horse is in the corral out back. Saddle's in the shed."

Maxwell fumbled with the buckles on one of the bags. He withdrew a sheaf of papers tied with string.

Trace leaned against the doorjamb of the open door with his rifle butt against his thigh, barrel pointed skyward, listening to the marshal and watching the street.

Loud snores started from the cell where Gus sprawled on the cot.

Maxwell cast him a glance then plunked his elbows onto the desk and cradled his head in his hands. He let out a moan. "My head's going to bust wide open." He looked up, his eyes bloodshot, and fumbled with the string holding the papers.

Cal stepped forward, popped open his pocketknife, and slit the twine for him.

The marshal blew his nose again on the red handkerchief and shuffled through the pages. "In the past six months, twenty-two kids have disappeared in Idaho and Montana territories."

Trace frowned and withdrew a toothpick from his shirt pocket and stuck it in the corner of his mouth. "Any connection between the kids? Anything similar as to age or whatnot?"

Maxwell shook his head then looked like he wished he hadn't. "Hard to say. Sadly, nobody took much notice at first. Not until a white kid from a respectable family was taken. The previous kidnappings were all of Chinese, Indian, and prostitutes' children. The one that got me a telegram from the territorial governor was a boy who got snatched right off the street in Silver City on his way home from school."

A heavy feeling spread through Trace's chest. Nobody cared until a respectable white child got taken? How did that matter? A child was a child, white or not. He could only imagine what the kidnappers wanted with children. He'd heard stories of children sold to brothels or to mine owners for cheap labor and worse.

Movement up the street caught Trace's eye. He immediately recognized the caramel-colored hair of Lily Whitman. She hurried across the street from the café and headed his way. His heart thumped a bit quicker, and he stilled his movements. She entered the doctor's office. Was she sick? No, more likely it was her sister, the pale girl with the baby. He'd only seen the other Miss Whitman a couple of times. She stayed hidden in the kitchen of the Rusty Bucket, as if she were afraid someone might notice her. Probably felt the sting of being a fallen woman in the eyes of the town.

Trace knew how public disapproval could hurt. McConnells weren't exactly high on the Money Creek society list. "So what do you have to go on?" Best to stick to what the marshal was saying.

The marshal started in on a coughing fit, his face going red and his eyes watering.

Cal sauntered to the stove and touched the side of the coffeepot. He shook his head as if the coffee wasn't hot enough and stirred the fire.

When the marshal could speak, he cleared his throat. "I got a message from a contact in Jardin, a guy I used to ride with and a steady hand with a gun, too. He heard a whisper from someone in town that for the right price a person could buy himself a kid. I've been chasing after these kidnappers, but here's a chance to get them to come to me."

"You got a plan?" Trace glanced at Maxwell then returned his gaze to the doc's place. Miss Whitman came out into the sunshine and headed up the street toward the general store. Trace's muscles tightened, and he straightened when he noticed a couple of miners staring after her, elbowing one another and laughing as she passed them. Maybe he should go have a word with those boys about how they behaved around the women of Money Creek.

"My associate should be here soon. A woman who works for the U.S. Marshals from time to time. The plan is for us to head to Jardin posing as husband and wife and hook up with my contact there. We'll set up a meeting to purchase a kid then follow the kidnappers from there to wherever they're holding the children." A paroxysm of coughing seized him, and he held his arms across his ribs.

Gus snorted and rolled over in his cell, tipping off the edge of the bunk onto the floor. He didn't move for a moment, and then his rhythmic snores began again.

Cal shot Trace a questioning look, and Trace shrugged. Experience told him it was no use putting him back on the bed. He'd just fall off again.

"And you want Trace along as an extra

gun." Cal hooked a chair with his boot and turned it to straddle it backwards.

"He's the best marksman in the territory, and he comes highly recommended. Colonel Bainbridge put in a good word for you with the governor."

Trace kept his expression impassive. Though he appreciated the colonel's support, it was high time he made his own way, proved his own worth, without trading on his relationship with Colonel Bainbridge.

Cal propped his chin on his stacked hands. " 'Scuse me for saying so, but you don't look like you're up to nabbing anything but a bed." Cal voiced what Trace had been thinking since the marshal first appeared. "Why don't you get some sleep until this associate comes in?"

Maxwell staggered upright with a groan and poured himself a mug of coffee. "I'm supposed to meet her on the westbound stage."

Trace palmed his watch. "Stage is due anytime now. I can fetch her."

The marshal set down his coffee cup, lurched to the first open cell, and collapsed onto the cot. "Much obliged."

Trace headed for the general store first. Wouldn't hurt to pick up some headache powders for the marshal on his way to the stage depot. He ignored the tingle on the back of his neck when he thought about seeing Lily Whitman again. He was just doing his job by checking up on her, looking out for a citizen of Money Creek.

He wished she hadn't chosen Purdy's Mercantile to do her trading in. Mrs. Purdy was known for her pompousness toward those she deemed undesirable. He hated to think of the store owner being rude to Miss Whitman on account of her sister. Though Mrs. Purdy had pulled in her horns considerably ever since Trace's sister-in-law, Clara, had laid into her awhile back for mistreating the McConnells, she could still cut a person down with her scythe-like tongue.

The bell jangled against the door when he entered, and the odors of spices and cloth and leather greeted him. He ducked to keep his hat from hitting the top of the doorway. Miss Whitman waited at the left-hand counter, fingering a bolt of lacy stuff. Mrs. Purdy's black dress rustled as she mixed something in a brown bottle. Miss Whitman's fingers trailed over the fabric, and a wistful sigh escaped her lips.

Mrs. Purdy added another teaspoon of liquid to the bottle. "Good thing I just got a new shipment of medicaments. You're really going through this cough syrup." Mrs.

Purdy held the bottle up, checked that the cork was in tight, and gave it a good shake. She glanced at Trace and stiffened. "Be with you in a moment."

Miss Whitman glanced up at him with those green-blue eyes, and his skin went hot. He shifted his weight, feeling like a jack pine in a rose garden, and swallowed hard. "No rush." He tipped his hat and turned to study the merchandise in a glass case on the counter. Heat raced up his chest when he realized he was staring at a display of ladies' nightwear. He backed away like he'd been bitten, and his rifle bumped into the pickle barrel. The brine sloshed, sending pungent fumes into the air.

Trace took a deep breath and stood stock still, regaining his control. "Guess I'll come back later." He touched his hat brim and ducked out of the store. Stupid idea going in there. Time to stop thinking about girls with turquoise eyes and get back to the job of being sheriff.

Lily stared after the retreating back of Trace McConnell. Whenever she encountered him about town or in the café, he never said a word he didn't have to, stoic as a cigar store Indian. Georgia doted on Trace's younger brother, Cal, but even that gregarious lady walked carefully around the new sheriff. It wasn't that he was scary really, just . . . she struggled for the right word . . . intensely controlled. Whenever she saw him, he made her think of a mountain lion — a very handsome mountain lion — all leashed power waiting to pounce.

"Here you go." Mrs. Purdy wrapped the bottle in a piece of brown paper and set the bundle upright on the counter. "That'll be thirty cents."

Lily carefully counted out two dimes and ten pennies. Her heart hurt a little to let the money go, but what could she do? Violet needed the medicine and that was that.

The morning sun glinted off the windows of the Rusty Bucket as Lily entered the café. Georgia sat at one of the tables with two customers, chatting and sipping coffee. She looked up when Lily passed by. "Lands, girl, where'd you come from? I thought you were upstairs with Violet."

"She needed some medicine. I stopped in at the doctor's office to see if he could come check on her, but he was out on a call. I left a note on his desk and went to the mercantile to get more cough syrup." She held up the paper-wrapped bottle. "If it's all right with you, I'll bring Rose down to the kitchen and feed her. She should nap this afternoon while I clean up from the lunch rush."

Georgia nodded. "I'll be in directly to peel the spuds. I just heard Violet on the back stairs, but she didn't come into the kitchen."

Lily headed to the loft. Violet rarely ventured downstairs these days, but maybe she'd gone to the privy. Did that mean she was feeling better or worse? Lily mounted the creaky stairs, but when she got to the landing at the top, the door hung wide open. Sobs greeted her before she ducked inside.

"Vi? Don't cry. I've got your medicine here. After you've had it, you can have a nice sleep." She stopped in surprise.

Violet lay in the middle of the floor, as if she'd fallen out of bed and tried to crawl to the stairs.

"Lily!" Violet gasped and coughed. "They took her! They took Rose."

Lily stooped to lift Violet back into the bed and glanced at the baby's crate, thinking Violet's fever must've brought on hallucinations. But the bed was empty. The string of spools lay on the floor.

Dread sliced through Lily. She helped Violet sit on the edge of the bed then went to check the crib again. "Who took Rose? The doctor? Was he here? I left him a note."

She grasped to understand. Surely the doctor would've told Georgia if he was going to take Rose to his office.

Violet sobbed again. "No, there were two men. I've never seen them before. They just came right in and grabbed her up." Her frail frame shuddered with chills. "Why? Why would they want my baby?" Red fever spots suffused her pale cheeks, and her eyes were glassy.

Fear for her and for the baby flashed in Lily's brain. "Lie down and get under the covers." She pulled the quilt over Violet, trying to think. "How long ago?"

Violet coughed and sobbed and shook her head. "Not long. Just before you came in."

"And there were two of them?"

"Yes. They had guns, Lily. One of them pointed his gun right at me." She clutched Lily's arm. "What are we going to do?"

Lily smoothed Violet's hair away from her face, her hand trembling. "You're going to lie still and try not to fret. I'll be back soon."

Lily clattered down the back steps once more and ran through the kitchen. "Georgia" — she skidded to a stop beside the table — "someone's taken the baby, and Violet's terribly sick. Can you go sit with her till I get back?"

Georgia leapt up with startling speed and

grace for someone of her size. "Took the baby? Who?" Like a giant mother bear, Georgia bristled.

"Two men. She didn't recognize them. That must've been when you heard the stairs creaking earlier. Please, I have to see if I can find them."

"Nonsense." Georgia gripped Lily's arm. "You're going to go right to the sheriff. Go get Trace. I'll see to Violet."

For a moment Lily stood rooted to the floorboards, her whole being resisting running to a man for help. She'd vowed never to need a man again, never to put her trust in such a fickle being who couldn't be counted on to keep his word.

Georgia gave her a push toward the door. "Get going, girl."

Lily ran up the street toward the jail, tears blurring her vision. Who would want to take the baby? Her mind went to Bobby Pratchett. But why would he want Rose now when he'd run away at the very idea of being a father? The last they'd heard he was somewhere up north working in the mines. He wouldn't come back for the baby now. Guilt swamped Lily. She'd promised Violet she'd look after Rose.

Lily reached the sheriff's office and stumbled inside.

The sheriff's brother, lounging in a chair tipped back to rest against the wall, thunked the legs of the chair down and stood. "Miss Whitman? Can I help you?" He smiled that smile that always flustered Georgia and got him extra slices of pie.

"I need the sheriff. There's been a kidnapping. Someone took my niece, Rose. She's just a baby." She gasped, blinking at her tears and putting her hand on her chest to keep her heart from leaping right out.

Something about the way the young man drew his sidearm and checked the load before putting it back in his holster reassured Lily. "How long?"

"Just a few minutes. I was at the mercantile."

"My brother's up the street at the stage office. Find him and send him to the café."

Lily bolted out the door before he finished speaking. She hurried to the small building that housed the Money Creek Stage Line.

Trace emerged as she approached, his brows drawn down, his rifle in his hand. He froze when he saw Lily, his face smoothing into a guarded expression. "Miss Whitman." He touched his hat brim.

"Sheriff, someone's stolen my niece, right out of her bed." She grabbed his arm and tugged.

"Stolen?"

"Yes, hurry. Cal's at the café now. Two men with guns have kidnapped Rose."

He stepped off the porch and started up the street.

Lily had to trot to keep up with his long strides, but she still urged him on. "Hurry, please."

THREE

Trace swept off his hat and ducked into the dim loft. He couldn't straighten up, not even in the center of the room where the roof was the highest. A single window provided a bit of light. The grim surroundings drew his mouth and brows down. An iron bedstead, a washstand, a few meager possessions.

What were two girls doing living alone like this, trying to care for a baby? Where was their family? He'd heard no mention of the baby's father. Maybe he was a drunk like Trace's pa. If he was, then the girls were better off without him, but they should have someone looking after them.

Faint, exhausted sobs came from the bed. Lily pushed past him and knelt beside the bed, stroking her sister's hair. "Don't cry, Vi. The sheriff's here. We'll get our Rose back." She shot Trace an imploring glance.

Cal hovered in the doorway, there being

no more room in the tiny space. Georgia, her face like a thundercloud, straightened the quilt on the far side of the bed.

Trace squatted beside the bed and rested his rifle across his knees. "Ma'am, can you tell me what happened?"

Violet sniffed and used the handkerchief Lily gave her.

Her pale face and the dark blue smudges under her fever-bright eyes took Trace right back to his own childhood, sitting beside his mama's bed in a ramshackle cabin. He heard again her shallow breathing and saw her sunken eyes and cracked lips, feeling as helpless now as he had then. The sight of the baby's empty bed jabbed him like a hot poker. His baby sister, Priscilla, hadn't been much older than the Whitman baby when the cholera took her and his mother both. He shoved down that memory and concentrated on the task at hand.

"There were two men. I couldn't stop them. They just barged right in and grabbed the baby. When I tried to get up, they laughed and one of them shoved me down." She started to cry again.

Lily patted her shoulder and looked up at Trace, tears hovering on her lashes. A giant fist grabbed Trace's chest and started squeezing.

Georgia grunted. "I heard the stairs creaking, but I thought it was Lily or Violet. I never even came up to check, just sat there drinking coffee with Seb and the boys downstairs, waiting for time to start serving lunch." Her voice was husky and thick. She wrung her work-reddened hands as if she'd like to have them around the necks of the kidnappers.

Trace nodded. "Hear any horses?"

Georgia shrugged. "Hard to tell. Horses coming and going all the time around here."

Trace motioned for Cal to go have a look-see in the alley. Cal ducked out and clattered down the stairs.

Lily's eyes blazed. "Who would do such a thing? And why? What could they possibly gain? A ransom? We don't have any money." Her lower lip disappeared behind her upper teeth, and though she stroked Violet's hair with one hand, the other lay in a tight fist in her lap.

Trace had the most ridiculous urge to comfort Lily, to tell her everything would be all right. But he couldn't promise that. Suddenly the badge he wore seemed to weigh a hundred pounds. He was the sheriff. He should be able to keep the citizens of his town safe.

Cal stuck his head through the door.

"Looks like a couple of horses were tied up in the alley. But they headed toward the main street." He and Trace shared a long look. If the men had ridden down the main street, tracking them would be nearly impossible. And if Maxwell was right, a posse would be useless against them.

"Saddle up. I'll be there soon."

Cal disappeared once more, his boots sounding on the steps.

A coughing spasm took hold of Violet, and she bent almost double, the bed creaking with each bone-jarring jerk. She clamped the handkerchief to her lips, and her tears scattered across the quilt on her knees. When she lay back, gasping, blood stained the square of cloth in her hand. Sadness seeped through Trace. The girl was a lung case, a bad one from the look of things. A shame.

"What did these fellows look like?" Trace knew Maxwell would be interested.

"A tall man with white skin and hair, almost bald." She stopped between words to gather breath. "And a short man, mean eyes. Bone-handled knife at his waist. He shoved me." Tears slipped out of her eyes — a paler version of her sister's — and tracked down her gray, hollow cheeks.

"Ma'am, don't try to talk anymore." Trace

started to rise, but Violet's thin hand gripped his arm. He instinctively covered it with his own. Her hot skin, paper-dry, reminded him of how his mother's hand had felt when she was dying.

"Please, get my baby back." She gasped and pressed her other hand to her frail chest as if to ward off the pain that must be slicing through her lungs. "Promise me."

He knew he shouldn't make that promise, but how could he deny her? "We'll get her back, ma'am. I promise."

Her hand fell away from his arm, and she closed her eyes. Trace nodded to Georgia and Lily and headed toward the stairs.

Lily's light step followed him. "You shouldn't have promised Violet you'd get Rose back."

He turned on the rickety stairs and found she was at eye level with him, two steps up. In a blinding flash, he remembered where he'd seen that exact color of green-blue. The ribbon. The hair ribbon his mama had treasured as one of her few precious luxuries. She'd stroked that piece of satin, smoothing it between her fingers before tying it around the end of the braid across her shoulder every morning. When the men from the mine came to burn the cabin and the cholera victims, Trace had fought like a wildcat to get that ribbon. He had sobbed, clutching the ribbon as the pyre went up — the only way to ensure the disease didn't spread. His pa had smacked him across the mouth and told him to shut up and be a man. Trace hadn't cried since. He'd kept that ribbon all these years, using it as a marker in his Bible.

He shoved the memories aside. "Why not?" She was right, but that was beside the point. He turned and headed toward the street. Cal would be here soon with the horses.

"Because in my experience, men don't keep their promises. They look for any excuse to break them." Desperation and doubt clung to her words, and a bitterness that seemed odd in one so young.

"I always keep my promises."

"That's what all men say." She glared up at him as she dogged his steps.

He sighed and kept walking. He had better things to do at the moment than palaver with a distraught woman in the middle of the street. "Go back upstairs and be with your sister." He marched away from her, but not before he heard her gasp of outrage.

Lily wrapped her shawl around her shoulders and trudged toward the jail. Light spilled from the windows of the Golden Slipper, casting blocks of light onto the dark street, while the piano tinkled a lively tune. Used to the noise from living next door to it for months, she gave the watering hole barely a glance. The sheriff and his brother had ridden past the Rusty Bucket moments before. Neither had been holding a baby.

Twin lanterns flanked the jail door, casing a yellow glow under the porch overhang. She blinked, steeling herself before stepping onto the plank stairs. Cold seeped into her fingers from the metal latch, and she had to put her shoulder into opening the sturdy door. She kept a tight rein on her thoughts, knowing that if she gave in to the heartache and fear, emotion would overwhelm her to the point that she couldn't function. She had to stay focused.

Trace emerged from one of the cells.

She stopped, her hand on the door. The very sight of the new sheriff both comforted and exasperated her.

He crossed the open space in two strides.

She glared up at him, hanging on to anger so she wouldn't dissolve into a teary mass. "Why did you come back without her? You promised you'd find her." The words seemed torn from her knotted throat. "I knew I couldn't trust you."

He gave no indication that her words penetrated his thick hide.

A groan turned her attention. A man lay on the cot in the cell where Trace had been. He thrashed, kicking off the covers. From the other cell, a deep, rhythmic snore began. Gus McConnell. But the other man — he moaned again then coughed, holding his chest.

A shaft of pain sliced through her at the sound, so like Violet's cough. "Who is he?"

Trace turned and reentered the cell. "Maxwell. He's a marshal. Rode in today."

"What's wrong with him?"

"He's sick."

Lily gritted her teeth. "I can see that. Is he consumptive?"

Trace bent to retrieve the blanket, tucking it around the marshal, whose face was bathed in sweat. "Naw, he's got the grippe. He's been working the kidnapping cases."

"Did you send for the doctor?" She stopped. "You said cases. More children besides Rose have been kidnapped?"

Before Trace could answer, the front door shut and Cal flipped his hat onto a peg. "Horses bedded." He rolled his shoulders. When he whacked his jeans, puffs of trail dust filled the air. "Miss Whitman." Cal unclipped his gun belt and wrapped it around

41

the holster. He laid it on the corner of the desk.

Lily recrossed the ends of her shawl and hugged them tight against her middle with her forearms. She turned to Trace. "Why did you come back? Shouldn't you both be chasing the kidnappers?"

Cal answered. "Yes, ma'am, but in case you hadn't noticed, it's pitch black outside. Can't track in the dark, and we didn't find any tracks to follow anyway. Looks like they hit the main road, and with the freight wagons heading up to the mines, their tracks just blended right in." He shrugged. "We figured it would be better to get back here to the jail to question Maxwell further. The marshal has an idea where they might be going."

Lily whirled, guilt and anger clashing in her breast. "Where? Are you leaving in the morning?"

Trace accepted a cup of coffee from Cal. "It's up to Maxwell when we leave. It's his case."

Cal eased past Trace to look at the marshal. "Think we should have the doc come down?"

The sick man opened his eyes. "McConnell" — his voice rasped — "you'll have to go in my place. Kidnappers won't stay in

Jardin long. Did you meet the stage?"

"Jardin? Is that where they're taking Rose?" Lily crowded into the tiny cell and knelt beside the cot. She took the handkerchief from her pocket and sponged the man's face. "Get me some water."

Trace helped her prop the marshal up, and Cal brought a cup of water. She held the cup to Maxwell's lips. After two swallows, he turned his head and sagged back. The pillow, a burlap sack over some corn husks from the sound of it, rustled and crackled under his head.

Cal rubbed the hair over his ear. "Marshal, the woman you were expecting, well, she won't be coming. Stage got robbed east of here." He clenched his fist. "Caught them on an uphill grade where they were slowed down. The woman was wounded. She's laid up and can't get here in time to do us any good."

"What woman? And what's in Jardin?" Lily dipped her handkerchief into the rest of the water in the cup and swabbed the marshal's neck. Their refusal to answer her many questions burned.

Trace edged past her and perched on the corner of the desk. He picked up his rifle and put it back down, as if he felt uneasy without it but could see no reason to have it in his hands at the moment. Cal sat down in a straight-backed chair and tilted it against the wall, hooking his boot heels on the stringer. When neither of them answered her, she set her jaw and marched out to the sheriff. "Well?"

He considered for a long time before speaking. "It's just possible the kidnappers are in Jardin. Some of them, at least. They're stealing children to sell them. The woman on the stage was going to pose with Maxwell as his wife and try to buy a kid."

Thoughts tumbled in Lily's head like blueberries being rinsed in a colander. Rose would be sold? Fear licked her insides. "And this woman isn't coming?"

"Guess not."

His brevity irked her. "What are you going to do? The marshal can't ride, not anytime soon. The kidnappers will get away, or they'll sell Rose to someone else and I'll never find her." Lily's voice rose in desperation. She gripped his arm. The warmth of his skin through his shirt seared her palm. How could he feel so warm and act so cold all at once? She allowed her hand to linger a moment longer before dropping it to her side.

He shrugged. "Looks like me 'n' Cal will have to head up there ourselves and see if we can get a line on things."

Cal cleared his throat. "I doubt anyone will mistake you and me for a married couple, Trace. You go nosing around up there as a lawman and you know what will happen."

Trace fixed his brother with a look. "You have a better idea?"

"How about we go through with Maxwell's plan? We just change the players." Cal tilted his head. "You and Lily can go as the married couple, and I'll take your place as the extra gun. You can buy Rose back, and then we follow the kidnappers to find the rest of the kids."

Lily blinked, trying to take in what he was saying, but before she could formulate a reply, Trace shook his head. "No."

"No?" Lily bristled, annoyed that he would answer for her so quickly.

"Why not?" Cal stood and shoved his hands into his pants pockets. "Maxwell must've thought it would work. He must figure it was the only way to get close to the kidnappers without raising suspicions, or he wouldn't have wanted to try it."

"It's too dangerous, that's why. She's not a trained officer of the law." He gestured toward Lily. "The woman Maxwell was waiting on has worked with the marshal's office before. She's a professional, and she knows the risks. Lily would be more hindrance than help. If we're chasing kidnappers, we won't have time to look after her, too."

"Now listen here" — Lily poked him in the shoulder — "don't talk about me like I'm not even here. And I can take care of myself. I don't need anyone to 'look after' me."

Trace stared at her hard.

She crossed her arms and stood her ground. If he thought he could intimidate her just because he was tall and strong and wore that badge, well, he had another long think coming. "You promised to get that baby back. You promised my sister. And what's more, I promised her, too. If you won't take me with you, I'll go to Jardin myself." The very idea took the starch out of her knees, but she refused to let Trace see any weakness in her. She'd show this arrogant lawman she didn't need his help or anyone else's.

Trace smoothed his mustache with the side of his finger. "You can't go, so stop thinking about it. Besides, who would take care of your sister while you're gone? She can't be left alone, sick as she is." He looked triumphant about coming up with a valid excuse not to take her along.

Lily's insides crumbled. Though she tried to control her voice, the words came out in a pain-wracked whisper. "Violet is dead. Rose is all I have left now. And I'll get her back with or without you."

FOUR

Lily allowed Trace to hand her up into the stage to Jardin. She glanced out the window to where Cal, mounted and leading Trace's saddled horse, headed up the street. He would meet them in Jardin later that night.

Several male passengers crowded into the cramped space inside the coach, and by the time Trace climbed aboard, the only seat left was directly across from her. He settled in, resting the butt of his rifle on the floor between his boots and leaning the barrel against the inside of his thigh. He leaned back and crossed his arms, his face stony.

She moistened her lips and tried to convince herself she wasn't intimidated. The moment the coach lurched into motion, her sister's funeral leapt into her mind. The ceremony had happened with what seemed almost indecent haste this morning. A few brief words by the preacher, a handful of dirt on a rough pine box, and it was done.

The only comfort to Lily came from the large, reassuring bodies of the McConnell brothers who flanked her as she buried her sister and the bone-crushing hug Georgia gave her.

After the service, Trace had told her to be ready to leave in an hour. Not wanting him to change his mind, she hadn't asked what had prompted his decision to let her go with him. Instead, she'd gone to her room and cried for her sister and her niece while she packed her bag.

Her mind drifted to the words the preacher had said over her sister's casket. *"And they that know thy name will put their trust in thee: for thou, Lord, hast not forsaken them that seek thee."*

God, I'm so alone. You've promised not to forsake me. I know that. But I can't seem to feel it. Help me to know You're near. Help me to know I'm not alone. And please, please, keep Rose safe until I can get to her.

What must the baby be going through right now? Had anyone fed her, bathed her? Was she warm? Had she already been sold to some stranger, someone Lily would never find? She pressed her tongue hard against the backs of her clenched teeth, searching for something to hold on to. At least the kidnappers had taken the blanket from the bed with the baby, probably to conceal her while they stole her away.

Lily clutched the reticule in her lap, feeling the lumps and bumps of Rose's favorite toy, remembering how the baby had loved to clack the spools together and gnaw on them. Lily resisted the urge to withdraw the string from her bag, hold it to her chest, and give in to the sobs aching in her chest.

The coach bounced, tossing her against the man on her left, breaking her free of her thoughts for a moment. "Oh, pardon me."

The passenger righted his bowler and straightened his tie, juggling the battered leather case on his knees. He grinned at her, a silver tooth sparkling from just right of center in his smile. "Worry not, *mon cher*. You are traveling alone?" She had to concentrate to cut through his heavy accent.

Before she could answer, Trace cut in. "No, she's not alone."

Lily frowned at him. It was the first time he'd spoken since ordering her not to speak to anyone on the stage and to let him do all the talking. All his talking wouldn't fill two minutes. Since they met, he'd done nothing but grunt, glare, and imitate a grizzly most of the time. His displeasure at having to take her along stuck out all over him like yucca spikes. If he was going to be so disagree-

50

able, why had he consented to bring her along in the first place? His steely eyes bored into hers as the coach bounced over the rough road.

She couldn't hold his look for long and turned her attention once more to the man beside her. She'd talk if she wanted to. "We're heading to Jardin. I've never been there before. I confess I've not heard good things about that settlement. It has a reputation of being rather a wild place, I understand."

The three other men in the stage, miners from the looks of them, guffawed and elbowed each other. "Wild? Ma'am, that place is woollier than a flock of sheep. Jardin's wide open and brawling every blessed hour of the day."

And the kidnappers had taken Rose there? The lump of fear she'd been trying to ignore swelled in her middle. "What about the law? Surely there must be someone to keep the peace there." Marshal Maxwell had been on his way to meet with a contact in Jardin. It seemed reasonable that the contact would be the town sheriff.

The oldest of the trio scratched his shoulder and sneered, showing brown teeth. "Law don't bother much with Jardin. They had a sheriff for a while, but he got hisself kilt a few months ago. Since then, folks pretty much do what they want." He nudged his buddy in the ribs. "What's a pretty gal like you doing heading to that rat hole for?" He licked his lips in a way that made Lily's skin crawl. "You wouldn't be a sportin' lady, would you? 'Cuz if you are, you're gonna cause a riot to break out in the streets. The men will empty the mines and empty their pockets for you, you're such a looker."

"She isn't a sporting lady." Trace's voice cut across the interior of the coach like a saber. He glared so hard at the miners that they all looked out the window as if fascinated by the scrub and rocky outcroppings flashing by.

Heat climbed Lily's cheeks and she glanced down self-consciously, stunned that these men would think such a thing of her — not only think it, but say it to her face. How many times in Money Creek had she warded off the advances of some man who thought she was a woman of loose morals? Just because her sister had made one error in judgment, had trusted the wrong man, their reputations were in tatters. It didn't matter that Lily was a good girl, as good as any in the town. She was guilty by association, and that was that.

She decided to ignore those uncouth men

and turn her attention to the businessman beside her. Perhaps if he went to Jardin often, he knew something of the town and its occupants. Anything she could glean might prove helpful in getting Rose back. "Are you heading to Jardin on business?" She smiled and ignored the low growl and recrossing of the arms going on in Trace's corner of the coach.

"*Oui, mademoiselle.* I will show you." The passenger took the opportunity to flip the latches on his case and open it wide on his knees. "I deal in firearms." Half a dozen bright handguns lay in red velvet niches inside the case — everything from a sinister, blue-metal Colt to an almost dainty, pearl-handled derringer no bigger than the palm of her hand. "Ze finest quality and ze best prices west of Chicago. Might you be interested in something for your personal protection? A lady cannot be too careful these days. Oh, but where are my manners?" With the dexterity of a faro dealer, he made a card appear. "Laurence Labec, newly of Montreal and formerly of Paris, at your service."

She took the card and smiled. "Thank you, Mr. Labec. I'm sure I don't know what I would do with a pistol. I've never even held a gun, much less fired one."

Mr. Labec needed no further encouragement. He took the derringer from its nest, checked to make sure it wasn't loaded, and offered it to her. "*S'il vous plaît.* As I said, you cannot be too careful. I have heard there are many stage robberies in these parts. You should have some way to protect yourself. This particular model is from *Monsieur* Remington. It holds two shots, of a .22 caliber."

She took the pistol partly because she didn't know how to graciously refuse and partly because she knew it would annoy Trace. She had a feeling he would have loved to stuff a gag in her mouth and toss her into the luggage boot for the remainder of the journey. "It's so light." The smooth handle and chased metal chilled her.

"It will weigh slightly more with ze bullets. You handle it well." He smiled, and his silver tooth flashed. "You are a natural. Ze gun, it was made for you. It is a perfect weapon for a handbag or a pocket, no?" Anticipation of a sale gleamed in Labec's eyes.

Trace's hand engulfed Lily's and removed the little pistol. "Perfect for a cardsharp's sleeve, you mean." With a casual flip, he tossed the gun back to the dealer, who scrabbled and caught it against his chest, the valise pitching on his knees for a moment. "The lady doesn't need a gun." Trace settled back and rested his hand on his rifle. He let the side of his coat fall open to reveal the worn handle of a revolver in a holster along his right leg.

"Of course, monsieur." Labec retreated, tucking the gun away and closing the case. He tried once more. "Would ze lady be so kind as to give me her name?"

Again Trace answered for her. "You can call her *Mrs.* McConnell."

Trace tipped his hat lower on his brow and pushed thoughts of gagging Lily to the back of his mind. If he'd known she was going to gab like an old woman the whole way, he never would've brought her along. Her look of shock when he'd called her Mrs. McConnell mirrored the feeling galloping through him. Like saying it out loud was different than the sideways manner in which they'd spoken about it while concocting this plan in the first place. He shook his head at her, cautioning her not to contradict him, and looked out the window.

A pretend wife. At least he'd gotten her to stop talking.

Not that it would make much difference to the men in the stagecoach or to the men of Jardin. Once they got a look at her, he'd have his hands full keeping them away from her. It was those eyes. They showed everything she was thinking or feeling just before it poured out of her mouth. And it didn't hurt that those green-blue messengers were fringed with chestnut lashes a shade darker than her hair, or that her lips were so pink and full. From the way she walked to the way she held her head, even the way she kept checking to make sure she kept her little bag close to her — everything about her was feminine and appealing.

Not to him, of course. He knew better than to let any woman skew his judgment. But to the male population of Jardin, she'd be like water in the desert. Those miners had it right — Jardin was a lawless rat hole. Trace ran his hand down the barrel of his rifle and pressed his elbow against the butt of his revolver. He hoped there wouldn't be gunplay, but he wasn't afraid of it, at least not for himself.

Lily sighed and closed her eyes, leaning her head against the back of the high seat. Her shoulders drooped a little. As spirited as she was, it was hard to remember how fresh her grief was. Sitting still like that, not talking for once, she looked harmless and a little fragile. But she had grit. He'd seen it in the set of her mouth, in the determined way she'd stood up to him when he first told her she couldn't come along.

But Maxwell had persuaded him in the end. "Those kidnappers won't stay in Jardin long. I don't know where their headquarters is, but it isn't Jardin. That's just a stopover. If you don't get up there fast, they'll disappear again. It might be months before we get another lead like this."

Trace had refused at first to consider taking Lily, even at the urging of Maxwell and Cal. Then he'd stood beside her at her sister's grave, remembering his own mother's funeral. Wishing he could comfort her but feeling helpless. When she looked him in the eye, it was all right there. She would go with or without him. The desire to help her get justice had waylaid his good sense.

Fool woman. He'd really had no choice but to bring her along with him. And who knew? This crazy plan just might work. Of course, that would mean she'd have to stop being so open and friendly about their business to every drummer and wayfarer they came across. The woman needed a keeper.

As was his custom, he went over his plan of action in his mind, trying to foresee every facet and anticipate any difficulties that might arise. He'd left Money Creek in good hands. He'd sent word for his brother Alec to come watch the town until Maxwell felt well enough to take over. It would only be for a few days at the most. In fact, if things went well, they might be able to make contact with the kidnappers as early as tonight and get the baby girl back. Then he could put Lily and Rose on the return stage to Money Creek, and he and Cal could chase the rest of the kidnappers without his having to worry about Lily.

No one spoke again until the stage rolled down the main street of Jardin. Trace guessed sleep was the only thing that kept Lily quiet. She roused when he leaned forward and shook her shoulder a bit. He couldn't help but smile a little at the way she blinked at him, trying to focus. For some strange reason, he had to resist the urge to stroke a stray tendril of hair off her cheek.

"Are we there?" She seemed to come aware all at once and stiffened, leaning away from him.

Since the coach had stopped in the middle of town, he didn't think her question needed an answer from him. He reached through the door and unlatched it, jumping down. His boots squished in the mud. She stepped into the doorway, and he put his hands on her waist, lifting her down and swinging her around to the boardwalk behind him to keep her out of the slop.

For a moment she kept her hands on his shoulders, almost at eye level. She glanced down where his hands still spanned her waist, and he let her go quickly as she stepped back.

He caught her valise from the driver and handed it to her, then reached back into the stage for his rifle. The last miner climbed down. When he looked past Trace and made a lewd comment under his breath, Trace turned and slammed the butt of his rifle into the man's soft stomach.

Lily turned when the man groaned and doubled over, but Trace gripped his gun and took her elbow, guiding her away from the stage.

Maxwell had given him the name of his contact. The sooner they met with him, the sooner he could get Lily inside and under cover.

From across the road someone whistled. Bawdy laughter tumbled from the saloons, six that he counted in the little stretch of road that passed for the main street. A scantily clad woman leaned out of her upper-story window and waved to a wagon of miners returning from a shift. They ignored her and stared at Lily instead.

A heavy weight pressed on Trace's shoulders. How was he going to keep her safe and rescue her niece at the same time?

FIVE

Lily allowed herself to be tugged along for all of thirty seconds then halted, yanking her arm from Trace's grasp and frowning up at him. One of her hairpins gave up the fight, and a hank of hair slid across her forehead and over one eye. She brushed it back, tucking it behind her ear. Exhaustion and worry made her irritable. "Must you run?"

He glanced skyward as if imploring the heavens for patience — something he seemed to do often. "It's coming on to dark. You need to be under cover before this town busts out."

As if to illustrate his words, a loud shout rocketed into the street from the doorway beside Lily, and a man flew backwards through the swinging saloon doors, arms flailing. The hitching post shuddered as the man plowed into it.

Lily let out a shriek and clutched Trace's

arm. In one fluid motion, Trace thrust her behind him against the wall and cocked his rifle. Lily peeked around Trace's shoulder, her heart racing.

Several men stood in the open doorway laughing and pointing, but no one followed the unfortunate bar patron into the street. The man hung on the hitching rail for a moment, shook his woolly head, then lurched up the step and back through the doors.

Lily pressed her palms into Trace's back, taking comfort from the warm muscles under the stretched fabric of his shirt. "You're squishing me."

He turned, picked up her valise, tucked it under his arm, and grabbed her hand. "Let's go."

Well, who bit him? He acted as if she had done something wrong. "Where are we going, if it isn't too much trouble to ask?"

"Church."

She gasped and would've questioned him further, but he silenced her with a look. What on earth could the man want with church?

The white frame structure at the end of the street caught her attention. It was the only decent-looking building she could see. Maybe it wasn't such a bad choice after all, though she didn't see how it would help them find Rose. In her limited experience, kidnappers didn't go to church.

The only occupant was a nearly bald man with a ragged scar from temple to chin like a lightning bolt across the left side of his face. He wore an outdated black suit and held a taper in his hand, lighting the kerosene lamps in their wall brackets. "Can I help you?" He had a pleasant baritone voice with a slight Southern drawl.

Trace dropped the valise, eased Lily farther into the room, and took one more look down the street before shutting the door.

Lily sank onto a pew, wearier than she could remember ever being. Her bones ached from the jostling, jouncing stage ride, and her eyes were so tired they rubbed like sandpaper every time she blinked. Her sleepless, sorrow-filled night bore down upon her fast.

Trace went to the window and scanned the road, though what he expected to see in the growing dusk, she didn't know. His gray eyes had a watchful, piercing look as he turned and assessed the man who continued to light lamps. "You seen the preacher hereabouts? Name of Greeley?"

The man went still, his hands dropping to

his sides. With a wary expression, he asked, "Why do you want him? He in some kind of trouble?"

"My business with him is my own. But he's not in any trouble that I know of."

For a long moment they squared off. Then the tension drained out of the man, and he smiled. "I guess you wouldn't have brought the lady if you were looking for trouble. Sorry about that. I'm Hart Greeley."

Trace gave no indication that this rough-hewn man's identity surprised him in the least, though Lily had never seen a parson who looked more like an outlaw than this one. She rubbed her forehead. Trace's perpetual calm frustrated her. The walls he threw up around himself were so high and thick, she wondered if he felt anything at all. His rigid control made her want to do something extreme just to get a reaction out of him.

If she weren't so tired, she'd think of something. She had to settle for frowning at his back.

"Marshal Maxwell sent me." Trace handed the man the creased paper. "Said you were the man to talk to about these missing kids."

Lily clambered to her feet. Why hadn't he told her? She glared at Trace for keeping her in the dark and held out her hand.

"Pastor Greeley, I'm Lily Whitman. One of the missing children is my niece. Have you seen her? Do you know where she is?"

The parson engulfed Lily's hand between his long, narrow fingers. "I'm sorry. I haven't seen any of the children. I don't know where they are."

Lily's heart fell. She looked to Trace, questioning him without words. If the parson couldn't help them, then they were wasting their time. The clock was ticking, and she didn't know if she could stand another night without Rose.

Before she could voice her concerns, the preacher spoke again. "I sent word to Maxwell after I overheard something in town. The source is a nasty fellow, but if there's anything underhanded going on in town, he knows about it. Wait here and I'll go find him." He turned and slipped out the side door of the church, moving with a grace and silence she wouldn't have thought possible for such a gangling man.

Trace went to the window and watched the street.

"What are you looking for?" She spoke so she wouldn't have to think about all the worry for Rose and grief for Violet behind the door of her heart. If she could focus on something else, maybe she could keep that door from opening.

He didn't look at her. "Cal. Should be here soon."

"Mr. Greeley's a rather unusual preacher." Lily yawned, almost apologized for her unladylike behavior, then decided against it. He wasn't paying any attention to her anyway. She was convinced that if she didn't goad him into conversation every once in a while, he wouldn't say a word to her all day. "I wonder what his story is. For a moment he looked like he thought you might arrest him or something."

Trace flicked a glance at her. "Maybe he was something else before he was a preacher. Maxwell trusts him. Guess we can, too, but don't go cozying up to him like he was your long-lost brother like you did with that fellow on the stage. Not everyone is as nice as I am."

She gaped at him, stung. "I did not cozy up to anyone. It's never wrong to be polite. I assume you'd rather I grunted at people or ignored them altogether like you do?"

"I'd rather you held your tongue."

Before she could form a suitable reply, the side door opened and Greeley returned. Following him was a small man wearing tattered brown pants and a faded shirt and jacket. Dirty gray hair flowed over his shoulders, and his bloodshot eyes darted like a rat's. He appeared shrunken in on himself, as if trying to hide in plain sight.

"This is Bobcat." Pastor Greeley tugged him forward. "He's the reason I wired Maxwell. Bobcat knows where we might be able to find the missing children."

Lily didn't know whether to be hopeful or to despair. If men like Bobcat had taken Rose, what must be happening to the baby right now? But this nasty little man before her might be her only hope of getting her niece back. She opened her mouth to question him, but Trace shook his head at her. Fine. He could start, but if he didn't get anywhere, she would have her turn.

Trace crossed his arms. "Tell what you know."

Bobcat swiped at his nose with the back of his hand and grimaced. He shifted the bulge in his cheek, revealing tobacco-stained teeth. "What's it worth to you?"

Menace shouted from every line of Trace's body. Lily shivered when he stepped forward, looming over Bobcat. "Depends on what you tell me. But know this . . . if you lie to me, I'll hunt you down like I would a hydrophobic skunk."

The pastor leaned his hip on the back of a pew and crossed his arms. "Bobcat, just tell this nice lawman what you know." A hint of steel sharpened Greeley's tone.

Lily wondered what hold the parson had over Bobcat, because Bobcat dropped his act and shrugged. "Figgers you'd be a lawman. Got peace officer stamped all over you." He glared at Trace under bushy gray brows. "I know where you kin get a kid. Couple of months back, a fella came into the saloon where I was drinking and put the word out quiet-like that they had some goods to trade. Being naturally curious, I inquired as to the type of goods. Thought maybe they had some liquor or guns or something. But it was kids. They're willing to sell kids to brothel owners or mine owners for slave labor or worse, or when it suits them, they pretend to be fixing up adoptions of orphans. They come through town regular, every month or so. They're here right now. As long as you're introduced by the right person, they'll deal with you."

"Who's the right person?" Lily couldn't keep the question from popping out. Trace frowned at her, but she stared right back. She wasn't a mere decoration on this mission to get Rose back, and she wasn't going to act like it.

Bobcat puffed up. "I am. I got close to them when I learned what they were doing.

I kin arrange for you to meet Brady. He's the one who handles the . . ." He scratched the side of his head and shifted the gob in his mouth again. "The transactions." A grin crossed his face as if he was pleased to have come up with the right word.

"When?"

"Best do it quick. They planned to leave sometime tonight. What do you want me to tell him?"

Hope surged through Lily. Tonight she'd hold Rose in her arms again. She had to blink back tears and swallow the lump in her throat.

Trace slid his watch out of his pocket and held it to the lamplight. "Tell them a couple wants a baby girl, less than a year old. Tell them we'll pay, but we want the baby tonight."

Bobcat nodded. "Won't be no trouble. Unless they don't got a baby girl like that."

"They do."

Bobcat shifted his weight, his fuzzy brows drawing together. "You're gonna have to be out in the open for a while so Brady kin size you up. You hole up here in the church, he's going to smell a rat." He scratched his collarbone. "Go have dinner at the café, like you would if you really was waiting in town to adopt a kid."

"This Brady is the ringleader? How many men does he have?"

"Dunno for sure. I get the feeling Brady answers to someone else, but I don't know who it is. He always has at least one man along and some gal to ride herd on the kids, but I don't know for sure how many he's got all told. Brady's slick. He don't show too much of his hand to anybody."

Trace nodded. Lily had dozens more questions, but she wanted Bobcat to be on his way to set up the meeting. She held her peace with difficulty.

Bobcat shrugged again. "Won't take me long to find Brady. But he won't be rushed. He'll have someone watching you from the minute I let him know you're in town. He ain't been in this business as long as he has without being careful. If he don't like the looks of you or if he gets wind you're any kind of a lawman, he'll bolt, and you won't find hide nor hair of that baby you're looking for."

Six

Trace ushered Lily into the restaurant with his hand on the small of her back. If what Bobcat said was true — and Pastor Greeley had assured him they could trust Bobcat in this issue if not in much else — then the kidnappers would have eyes on them right now. They had to act like a married couple. Though he didn't have the foggiest notion how.

Lily didn't seem to either. If she stood any stiffer, her spine would crack. Every eye in the place turned to look at her as they wove through the diners to an empty table. He reached for her chair at the same time she did, and for a moment they had a tug-of-war. She looked at him like he was daft, her brows drawn down over her nose. "Fine, I'll take the other one."

"Lily, I'm trying to hold your chair for you."

She stood still, her eyes widening, then

plopped onto the seat. "I'm not used to men doing things for me."

He sat opposite her and laid his rifle across his knees. He leaned forward to whisper, "You heard what Bobcat said. Folks will be watching our every move from now until the meeting. We have to act like we're married. I've seen my brother Alec hold his wife's chair for her. Figured it wouldn't hurt." He leaned back as a thin, wiry woman slapped two coffee cups and some cutlery on the table.

"Got split pea soup tonight and rabbit stew. Biscuits are extra, but the coffee comes with the meal." The stuff she poured out of the spatterware pot might have been coffee once but now resembled axle grease. He picked up his cup and blew across the brew, half expecting it to smell of tar. At least it was hot. "We'll both have the stew and biscuits."

Lily loosened the strings on her bag and let it drop to her lap. "I can order my own food, you know."

"Quit scowling at me. A 'wife' shouldn't look at her 'husband' that way." He sipped his coffee, keeping his eyes above the brim of his cup to scan the crowd. Rough miners, teamsters, townsmen, and not a woman among them. Guess the womenfolk of Jardin knew better than to be out after dark. The need to protect Lily ratcheted up a notch.

"From what I've seen, being married lends itself to a lot of scowling." Lily leaned forward to peer into her cup but didn't appear brave enough to sample it.

Trace grunted. "Maybe we can get you some water. This stuff tastes like it was stirred with a horseshoe." He lowered his voice and leaned closer so no one would overhear. "Are you against marriage?" What woman would be against marriage? Wasn't every female looking for a husband from the minute she drew a breath?

"No, marriage is all right for *some* women." She picked up her knife and scrutinized it, her lips twisting as she laid it aside. "Georgia would have a fit at the state of this place and be after it with a mop and some hot water before you could drop one of these dirty utensils."

"Georgia does like things tidy. Don't you want to get married someday?" His curiosity surprised him. His policy most times was that other people's business and feelings were their own and not his to pry into. But it didn't make sense for a girl as pretty as Lily Whitman not to want to get married. And he had to go after what didn't make sense until it did. She'd make someone a nice little wife . . . as long as that fellow didn't mind her chattering. "Who's going to take care of you if you don't get married? Isn't there a pa or brother to see after you?"

"I don't need a man to take care of me." Her tired eyes snapped to life, all blue-green fire. "I can take care of myself, thank you. Men can't be trusted to take care of women. They say they love you and will take care of you, they promise the moon, and then before you know where you are, they're gone or kicking you out of the house, and you're left to fend for yourself."

Anger on her behalf blazed up his chest. "Did someone do that to you? Someone promise to marry you and then run off?"

She shook her head. "Not me. Violet." Her voice thickened, and he thought she might cry. Though he didn't know what he'd do if she did burst into tears. He almost blew out a sigh of relief when she got angry instead. "She trusted a man, and look what it got her — a baby but no wedding. A bunch of promises that turned out to be a pack of lies. Sorrow and shame so big that it weakened her mind and body until it finally killed her. Oh, and let's not forget her father. . . ." She leaned forward, her hands gripping the edge of the table until they shook. "The man who was supposed to protect and love her no matter what. Our father, bakery owner and respected businessman of Boise, was so concerned for his reputation that he kicked Violet out without a penny to her name the minute he found out she was in the family way. It was the dead of winter, and he knew she had weak lungs, too. When he turned his back on his own daughter, I left home with her. I'd rather live on the street than abide with such an unforgiving and hurtful man."

Trace reached over and loosened her hand, cradling it in his. "That's how you ended up in Money Creek? What happened to the baby's father?" The cramped loft they'd been living in came to his recall. Barely getting by working in the café kitchen, taking care of a baby and a consumptive sister. No one to care for them, to protect them and see that they were looked after properly. He admired her grit. Not many women would've left the comforts of home to look after a sister whose character had taken such a blow.

"Bobby Pratchett lit a shuck for the hills when he found out Violet was carrying. He went so fast he was just a puff of smoke on the horizon before Violet even knew he was gone."

"Maybe when we get back to Money Creek, I could locate this Bobby Pratchett and make him face his responsibilities." He rubbed his thumb across the back of her hand, feeling the bones, light as a bird's. "A man shouldn't run out on his family like that." Though that was all Trace had known his whole life — his father running from responsibilities straight into the bottom of a whiskey bottle.

"Don't bother. I don't want Bobby to have anything to do with Rose. I may not be much family for her, but she's better off without him." She withdrew her hand and let it fall to her lap.

"What about your ma?"

"She died when I was nine."

"And you been taking care of Violet ever since?"

Tears filled her eyes. She blinked and lifted her chin. "Enough about me. What about you? Are you planning on getting married?"

Trace wasn't ready for the switch in topics, though by now he should've been. She could hop tracks faster than a flea could swap dogs. He sat back and steadied the gun on his knees, scanning the room, wondering which man might be a kidnapper. "No, ma'am. Not me."

She crossed her arms and pressed her lips while narrowing her eyes. "Isn't that just like a man? You think women have to be married, that we all need protectors, and yet you're only too happy to exclude yourself from the responsibility. It's necessary for everyone else but you? What makes you so special?"

A hound dog couldn't have treed a raccoon more easily. He blinked and just managed not to squirm under her disapproving stare. Avoiding her eyes, he swallowed hard and smoothed his mustache, grateful that the waitress butted in with their dinners.

The woman dropped two plates of stew in front of them and shuffled away.

"There's men that are cut out for it, and there's men that aren't. I'm one that isn't."

She regarded him skeptically then picked up her fork. He followed suit and poked at the greasy brown mass steaming gently before him. A lumpy biscuit perched on the rim of his plate, and he picked it up, hoping it didn't taste as dry as it looked.

"Why aren't you?"

"Why aren't I what?"

Her fingers drummed the tabletop. "Why aren't you cut out for marriage? I'd think, as a lawman, you'd be a natural fit. Bossy, rule-oriented, used to getting your own way . . ."

"That doesn't follow. A man can be a good sheriff without wanting to get married. Besides, who'd marry a McConnell anyway?"

"Clara Bainbridge. She married your brother, and he's a McConnell." She challenged him while crumbling her biscuit into her stew.

"Clara's different, and so's Alec. The exceptions that prove the rule. But no other woman in Money Creek would risk taking on a McConnell. You've seen how my pa is. I'd rather stay alone all my life than marry a woman and break her heart like my pa broke my ma's." He jabbed a lump of stew. "Quit your jawing and eat up."

"You're doing your share of the talking," she muttered.

He tried to ignore her probing gaze but caught it anyway, and he had to admit she was right. He'd talked more in the last ten minutes than he did most days. The thought disturbed him.

"Are we going to wait for Cal? And does he share your views about McConnells marrying?" Lily toyed with her fork, twirling it on one tine on the rim of her tin plate but not eating.

He should've known she couldn't go two

minutes without talking. "Open your eyes, girl. He's sitting in the corner watching us. And yep, he doesn't want to get married any more than I do. Though he does enjoy feminine attention. Girls are usually falling all over themselves for his favor." The stew tasted nothing like rabbit — or anything else Trace could identify — so he let his fork fall.

Lily turned her head slightly toward where he flicked a glance.

Cal tipped his chair against the wall and hooked his boot heels around the legs. He cradled a cup of coffee on his stomach, his hat pulled down low. His eyes gleamed like a wolf's in the shadow of his hat brim. Trace didn't relax his vigil, but he did feel better with Cal on guard. Not much got past his little brother.

The door opened and Bobcat edged in. He scanned the room, and when his eyes lighted on Trace, the filthy man jutted his chin out and jerked his head toward the door.

Trace swallowed the last of the thick, bitter coffee. "Time to go."

This time she let him help her with her chair, her face going pale as milk and her hands shaking.

He wished she were well out of this situation. The sort of men they were going up against, men who would pull a baby from its mother's arms to sell for profit, wouldn't hesitate to abuse or even kill a woman who got in their way.

SEVEN

Lily could barely make out Bobcat ahead of them in the darkness. She stayed close to Trace, reassured by his silent tread and the solid heft of the rifle he carried. If she closed her eyes, she was sure she could make out the imprint of every single one of his fingers on her elbow.

Lily blinked and shook her head. *Keep your mind on the business at hand and get it off Trace McConnell and how glad you are that he's with you.*

Bobcat didn't speak, shuffling along until they stood in an alley beside the hotel, the only two-story building in town. His eyes glittered in his dirty face when he stopped and turned to put his back to the wall. "I done what you said." His whisper rasped across Lily's skin. "The folks you want to talk to are in the room at the head of the stairs. Two men. One of them watched you for a while in the restaurant. They have the kid with them in the room." He hovered expectantly, shifting his weight on the balls of his feet. He flinched when a hand came out of the darkness and descended on his shoulder.

Lily stifled a gasp.

Cal stepped close and let his hand fall away from Bobcat, who cringed and scowled. Cal pushed his hat back. "Circled the building. There's a back door. Nobody watching that I could see."

Bobcat cast a quick glance up the alley. "Who're you?"

"Never you mind." Cal smiled encouragingly to Lily. "Hello, Miss Lily. You're looking fine tonight." He pointed with his thumb toward the front of the building and addressed Trace. "I figure I'll loiter at the bottom of the stairs in the front room. That way I can see both doors and the head of the stairs."

Lily's hands shook, and she clamped them together. Rose was so near. It took all her self-control not to run into the hotel and demand that the kidnappers give her niece back. She focused on Bobcat. "You saw the baby? Is she all right?"

He shrugged as if the child were of no consequence. "They had the kid wrapped up. Didn't get a good look at her. Seemed fine."

Lily wanted to smack him. At least the kidnappers had Rose wrapped against the night chill. Lily rubbed her hands on her upper arms, hugging herself, anxious to get moving. "Are we going soon?" She poked Trace in the side.

"Best to know all we can about what we're up against. You got anything else?" He motioned with his rifle toward Bobcat.

"Like I said, two men. And no guns. You can't go in heeled. Oh, and I hope you got cash."

Trace nodded. "I understand." He flipped a coin toward Bobcat. "Thanks for your help. Now make yourself scarce."

His calm certainty steadied Lily, and his determination to keep his promise to Violet to get Rose back showed in his careful planning and single-mindedness. Then she frowned, chastising herself. As many times as she'd been hurt in the past, she should know better than to put all her trust in a mere man.

Trace handed Cal his rifle and unbuckled his gun belt. He removed the revolver from the holster and stuck it into the back of his pants under his coat. "I won't go in loaded for bear, but I can't go in there without something."

"Let's go." Lily tugged on his sleeve.

"Fine, but you let me do the talking." He scowled at her. "If I could figure a way to keep you out of this, I would. You just keep quiet, let me do the negotiating, and we'll get your niece out of there. Don't do anything but stand there. If we spook them, they might start shooting. The last thing we want is for bullets to start flying in that cramped hotel room."

She decided not to take exception to his telling her once again to keep her mouth shut. As if she'd do anything to jeopardize Rose's safety. Later, after the baby was safe, he'd hear what she thought of his high-handed opinions.

A weedy-looking man hovered behind the counter in the front room of the hotel. Trace took Lily's elbow and headed her to the stairway, not stopping to speak to the clerk. Damp spots showed on the bead-board ceiling, and a musty smell pervaded the hotel. Cal took up a post leaning against the wall near the front door, cradling Trace's rifle and looking at his watch as if waiting for someone.

The stairs creaked, and the threadbare runner crunched with grit and sand. A lone lantern sconce cast sickly yellow light down the dark hallway. She looked long into Trace's eyes as they stood side by side in front of the door, drawing strength. With a small nod, he reassured her. Determination hardened his gray eyes, giving him a bird-of-prey look. Lily shivered, glad he wasn't on her trail. Trace knocked.

The door opened a crack, and a ghoulishly pale man peered out. Wispy strands of white-blond hair hovered over his head. He looked them up and down with a fishy eye then pulled the door wider.

A single lamp, turned low, illuminated a corner of the room. The only other light came from the window where the lace curtains filtered the star-shine and kept it close to the panes.

Lily's attention went to the covered basket on the end of the bed. It moved slightly, and a tiny snuffling sound came from under the blanket. Rose's blanket that Lily had made for her. A lump grew in her throat to have Rose so near.

"I'm Mr. Brady. We don't normally handle business in this rather clandestine way, but your contact said you were in a hurry, and so are we. If you'll be so kind to produce the necessary money to cover the transaction fees, we'll effect the adoption."

Lily swiveled to stare, fascinated. She

never expected such a rich, mellow voice to come from such a cadaverous-looking man.

He brushed the tips of his fingers across his pate, languid and light. He looked more like an undertaker than a kidnapper, though she had to admit she'd never actually seen a kidnapper before.

"How much?" Trace turned slightly, and only then did Lily realize there was another man in the room.

This smallish, buckskin-clad fellow leaned against a dressing table. A slow scrape sent a shiver up Lily's neck. He drew a wicked-looking knife against a sharpening stone, turning the blade. He paused to spit on the stone before resuming the soft grinding.

"Two hundred. Gold."

Trace's lips flattened, and he rubbed his mustache as if deep in thought. "That's a lot of money."

Lily stiffened, her already-tense muscles going tighter. How dare he jeopardize things by dickering! Hot words crowded up her throat, but Trace flicked a stern glance at her, reminding her to keep quiet. She shook from the effort. Why was he dithering and hanging about? *Just give them the money so I can have Rose back!*

A fruity chuckle escaped the pallid kidnapper. "You are correct, but I'm afraid I cannot bargain. Caring for orphans as we do requires quite a bit of capital. Children aren't cheap. The transaction fee we charge allows us to feed and clothe the other foundlings in our care until we can find homes for them."

His bold-faced lie rolled from his tongue like syrup, and he inclined his head toward them as if petitioning them to understand his quandary. "I'm afraid my hands are tied in the matter. My superiors require the full amount to be paid in gold at the time of the transfer."

"We might be in the market for a boy, too, about seven or eight. Need some help on the farm. I'd have taken a boy right away, but the wife had her heart set on a baby girl. Do you have a discount if we take two kids?"

His long face got even longer. "I wish I had known you might be interested in more than one child. I'm afraid my colleagues have taken the rest of the children on ahead of us."

Trace shrugged as if it were of no consequence. "Maybe next time you're through this way, we can get a boy from you. You come often?"

Like the sun peeking over the horizon and lighting the landscape, Lily suddenly understood what Trace was doing. She had to admire the way he tried to draw information from the kidnappers. But her hands still itched to snatch Rose and run.

Trace's hands itched to punch the washed-out kidnapper right in his hooked nose. The abomination of selling children — children stolen from their beds, from the very arms of their dying mothers — made bile rise in Trace's throat until it burned. But he had to stay calm. He was a farmer looking to adopt a baby. Time enough when all the children were safe to exact some justice on the kidnappers.

He could almost feel the impatience rolling off Lily in waves. So far she'd managed to bite her tongue, but he wondered how long she'd be able to keep from talking.

The fellow in the corner, the one with the knife, bothered Trace. He'd seen him somewhere before. Hanging around one of the saloons in Money Creek? Maybe. If trouble was going to come, it would come from him. Trace angled his body another couple of inches to put himself between Lily and that blade. He took care to memorize the man's face and made note to check the wanted posters in the desk drawer in the jail as soon as he got home.

"Quit palavering." The knife went into a sheath at the man's side. "We've got to be getting on. Either you've got the money or you don't." He dug in his pocket for a pouch and dipped out a wad to tuck into his cheek.

"Don't you have some documents for us to sign? Adoption papers?"

Trace didn't miss the look between the two men. Brady nodded. "I'm afraid the forms have traveled on with our colleagues and the other children. However, I would be willing to post them back to you when we reach our next destination."

Probably didn't want to leave a trail. "Where is that next destination? Maybe I can ride over for them."

"Enough questions. You want the kid or don't you?" The man in the corner stepped close enough that Trace could smell the tobacco on his breath. "Time's wasting."

Lily gripped Trace's arm. He'd pressed them far enough. Digging in his inside coat pocket, he withdrew a pouch and tossed it to the bald man. "Two hundred in gold."

Brady loosened the string closure and peeked inside, his eyes coming to life for the first time as his bony finger stirred the coins. He lifted the basket by the handle and passed it to Lily.

Lily cradled the basket, her eyes huge in the low lamplight. Tears glistened on her lower lashes.

Trace swept the room once more then nodded. "Much obliged." He ushered Lily down the stairs. With barely a nod to Cal, he hurried their steps out of the hotel and onto the street. "Head toward the church. Pastor Greeley said to go to the parsonage just behind there once we had the baby."

Lily nodded, the tears tracking down her cheeks.

A feeling of satisfaction and accomplishment surged through Trace. If nothing else, he'd kept his promise to both Lily and her dead sister. They'd gotten Rose back. He put his arm around Lily's shoulders and guided her up the road.

Pastor Greeley opened the door to them before Trace could knock. "We've been on pins and needles waiting for you. This is my wife, Mei Lin." A tiny Asian woman half Greeley's size stepped forward.

"Please, come in. You were successful in rescuing the baby?" Lamplight ran along her glossy black braid shot through with gray hairs. Fine wrinkles lined her oval face and lent an air of wisdom and strength to her small frame.

Lily stepped forward, clutching her precious burden. Her eye shone in a way that made Trace's heart feel warm. She sat in the chair Greeley pulled out for her and began to unwrap the blanket.

Trace pulled the gun from the small of his back and checked his load. He'd get his rifle back as soon as he caught up with his brother. "I'm going to go after them. Cal will be trailing them to see where they go. We'll size up the situation and see if we can't get at least the two who were there tonight."

Plans rolled through Trace's mind. If they took down the kidnappers they'd met tonight, surely one of them would break and give them some information on the rest of the gang. Trace would be able to take that information to Marshal Maxwell.

He even allowed himself a moment to consider how good it would feel to return home with Lily and Rose. People would respect him then, because they'd see with their own eyes he was a good lawman. Perhaps the McConnell name in Money Creek would mean more than a shiftless drunk and his maverick sons. But time enough for all that after he'd gone to help Cal.

A squawk from the baby mingled with a gasp from Lily.

Trace stopped, his hand on the door latch. "Oh no."

He glanced over his shoulder into Lily's stricken eyes. "What? Is she hurt?" A cold fist wrapped around his heart and squeezed. If those monsters had injured that baby, he'd hunt them till they dropped.

Lily shook her head and blinked.

"Then what?"

"This isn't Rose."

EIGHT

He left.

Just like a man.

The thought ricocheted through Lily's mind as she stared at the closed door. Her thoughts reeled with shock. All her hopes, all the excitement and the joy at having her niece back in her arms, burst like soap bubbles. She looked down into the face of the infant, cataloging the shock of black hair, the dark eyes, and the high cheekbones — the instantly recognizable features of an Indian baby.

Pastor Greeley crouched beside Lily's chair and caressed the child's head. His hand dwarfed the baby, but she didn't cry. Instead, tiny fingers came up and clasped a gnarled knuckle, rosy lips splitting in a grin that sent drool sliding over chin and bare chest. He chuckled when the baby tried to gnaw on his finger. "She's a pretty little thing."

The baby squealed and squirmed. Lily adjusted her grip automatically, her mind numb. What did it matter that this child was pretty, when she wasn't Rose?

Mei Lin stirred the coals in the stove and lifted a bucket of water to fill a pot to warm. "Right baby or not, this one needs a bath and clean clothes. Hart" — her hand rested on Greeley's shoulder — "we will need more water and wood."

The pastor unfolded his long frame and went to do his wife's bidding.

Lily sat frozen. It wasn't supposed to be this way. She should be holding Rose, hugging her niece, kissing her chubby cheeks, stroking her almost nonexistent fluffy pale hair.

"I will take her." Mei Lin held her hands out for the infant.

Lily let the baby go, her arms falling empty to her sides. That emptiness spread through her, pushing tears from her eyes in a steady stream. To come so close hurt more than she could've imagined. She should've known better. Better than to hope, to expect her trust to be rewarded.

God, I trusted You. I trusted You to bring Rose back to me.

Frigid loneliness swept over Lily. Violet was gone, Rose was still missing, and Trace

94

had disappeared into the night. She had no one.

"Hello, sweet baby." Mei Lin finished unwrapping the baby on the table. Pudgy legs flailed in the air, and a decidedly ripe smell made Lily wrinkle her nose. The older woman placed her hand on the baby's tummy and held her there while she tested the water in the basin she'd placed on the table. "We'll have you cleaned up soon." Her voice lilted, capturing the infant's attention.

Though it went against everything in Lily to sit idle while someone else worked, she couldn't seem to rouse herself to help. Devastation fixed her to her chair.

"Hart told me of your search for your little girl. I am sorry things did not go as you had planned." Mei Lin swiped the baby with the wet cloth, wrinkling her nose when the washrag came away streaked with grime. "But do not give up hope."

Hope. Until this moment, Lily had always had hope. Hope of a brighter future for herself and for Violet and Rose. Hope that someday she would have the bakery she dreamed of, a secure financial future, and her sister and niece to be all the family she needed. Hope that God would reward her trust in Him and His faithfulness. She'd never questioned His goodness before, but as disappointment and disillusionments piled up around her, she found her faith growing thin, her grasp on hope more tenuous.

Pastor Greeley returned with an armload of wood and a pail of water. His frown puckered the scar on the side of his face. "Some miners are painting the town a very vivid shade of red tonight. You girls make sure you stay inside and out of sight." He stacked the wood in the box beside the stove and poured the contents of the bucket into the reservoir to warm.

"Do you think Trace will be gone long?" Lily forced the question past her stiff lips. Would he come back at all? And how would she ever find Rose if he didn't?

"Depends on what he finds. Trace McConnell seems like one man I wouldn't want on my trail; but if he gets too close and feels the other children are in danger, he'll back off and regroup."

Lily took heart at the pastor's words. "You still think he'll find her?"

"That I do. I hear things, even in a backwater like Jardin. Trace McConnell is a hard man, an excellent shot, and an expert tracker. And from what I've seen here even tonight, he looks like a man who won't quit until he gets what he's after."

She shook herself, struggling to throw off her inertia. Sitting here wasn't accomplishing anything. She always thought better when she was working, and she needed to formulate a plan to get Rose back, with or without Trace's help. If he came back, fine, but she wouldn't quit. The first step to finding Rose was to stop sitting there like an old dust rag. "What can I do to help?" If she could keep her hands busy, perhaps she could tamp down some of the anxiety clawing up her throat.

Mei Lin wrapped the baby in a coarse towel and handed her to Lily. "Hold her, and I will see what I have to clothe her in." She disappeared into another room. Sounds of rummaging and the creak of a cupboard door or a trunk lid came through the doorway.

Lily dried the baby, careful to get into the deep creases under her chin and into the rolls on her chubby thighs. The child might have been dirty and in need of a fresh diaper, but at least she hadn't been starved. Were they feeding Rose as well? A hard lump formed in Lily's throat and tears stung the inside of her nose. She sniffed and blinked hard.

Pastor Greeley sat at the table. He turned

a page in his Bible. The rustling of the onion paper reminded Lily of sitting in church as a little girl when her mother would help her find the right page. Without looking up, he said, "Sometimes it's hard to trust, isn't it? That God hears you and knows what you're going through?"

Lily started, wondering how he had read her mind.

A small smile tugged at the corner of his mouth, the side with the scar. "I don't know your story, and I can only imagine how you're feeling right now." He adjusted the half-moon glasses on his nose and reached out to turn up the flame on the lamp before him. "But you're going to have to trust, trust both God and Trace to work on your behalf."

Before Lily could sift through his words, Mei Lin emerged from the other room and held up a chemise. "This is the best I can do. I have no clothes for one so small. Perhaps, Hart, you will go shopping in the morning?"

He nodded and continued reading as if looking for something specific.

Lily sat opposite him and helped Mei Lin slide the baby into the chemise. Her father never would've gone to the mercantile for baby clothes, or for any other household goods for that matter. Shopping was a woman's duty and beneath a man. "It's hard to picture you shopping for baby clothes. Are you sure you wouldn't want me to go instead?"

"Not into Jardin. Not alone. It wouldn't be safe. In case you didn't notice, there aren't too many women in town, and most of those that are . . ." He paused as if searching for the right word. "They're saloon girls. You can't walk around town without a man to protect you. Some miner or teamster might get the wrong impression and make an improper advance. Things are sticky enough as it is. As long as you stay here, though, there shouldn't be any problems. The men of the town know better than to cause trouble around the church, but there's no sense tempting them with a lady as pretty as you are."

A hot blush started somewhere along Lily's neckline and rose in a rush up her cheeks. Being the sister of a fallen woman had garnered her more than enough improper advances over the past few months in Money Creek. Violet had warded off more than one lascivious lout, and finally she'd taken to staying in the kitchen or the tiny loft they shared. Lily refused to let their boorish manners make her run and hide, though she was careful not to encourage them in any way. But the thought of not even being able to walk the aisles of the local general store without being accosted sent shivers up Lily's spine.

Pastor Greeley leaned back and crossed his legs. His coat fell away from his side, revealing a gun in a holster. What kind of parson went around armed? He noticed her staring and a chuckle escaped his lips. "I've found carrying a sidearm and a Bible deters a lot of mischief. And don't you worry. I know how and when to use both."

Lily blinked and couldn't resist glancing at the clock on the wall. If only Trace would return with news.

Trace gripped his revolver until his knuckles ached. With growing dread he eased around the corner of the hotel. Cal's horse was still at the livery stable, so he must be in town somewhere. But where?

Raucous laughter spilled from the saloon next door, along with the smells of red-eye and cigar smoke.

Worry and shame dogged Trace every step of the way. The stricken look in Lily's eyes when she unwrapped that baby and found it wasn't Rose . . . He'd carry that look for the rest of his days. He'd failed her. Served him right for being so arrogant, imagining the welcome home parade and praise of Money Creek when he returned victorious. He could barely admit to himself that the person he had most wanted to please was Lily herself, to hear her words of praise, to see admiration in her pretty eyes.

Where had his plans jumped the track? A bitter gust of air came from his lungs. Since the moment Lily got involved, if he recollected correctly. From the minute he'd agreed she could come along, he hadn't been thinking worth a plugged nickel. Methods that had proven themselves time and again in the past had failed. Lily had him buffaloed to the point where he couldn't even count on the one ability that had always stood by him — his ability as a lawman.

He shook his head to clear her from his thoughts so he could concentrate. Mooning about a woman while tracking kidnappers was a sure way to get himself killed. Trace didn't fancy getting a Bowie between the ribs, and that knife-wielding fellow in the hotel room looked like he'd done his share of dry-gulching men in dark alleys.

As if the thought gave life to the image, he rounded a pyramid of empty whiskey kegs behind the saloon and stopped cold. A familiar figure sprawled facedown in the rutted dirt. Trace's mouth went dry. For a long moment he couldn't make his boots move. At last he edged forward, revolver at the ready, knowing what he would find.

Cal's hat lay a few feet away, his hand outstretched on the ground as if reaching for it. Trace crouched beside his brother, regret and grief pressing on him. He should've protected him. He should've known how dangerous it was to get too close to the kidnappers. He should've been the one to follow after them.

Anger flared in his chest against the men who had done this. Trace made a silent vow to follow the kidnappers for the rest of their born days. They would pay for this and their other foul deeds.

He didn't realize he'd closed his eyes against the pain and loss until a groan made his lids pop open. Surprise and relief surged through him when Cal stirred and moaned again. "Cal!" Trace eased his brother over.

Blood trickled down Cal's temple, and his eyelids flickered. He grimaced and put his hand against his head.

Trace helped him sit up but stopped him when he tried to rise. "Hold on there. What happened? Where are you hurt?" He ran his hands over Cal's torso, searching for bullet or knife wounds.

"Head." He blinked hard then looked around him. "Where're my guns?"

Trace cast about, picking up Cal's hat, and though he hadn't expected to find the weapon, he felt a surge of relief when his boot hit something that proved to be his own rifle that he'd given to Cal before entering the hotel. Cal's revolver lay near his hat.

"Was carrying both guns when someone hit me from behind." His voice sounded stronger, tinged with disgust and anger.

"Any idea who did it?" Trace grabbed Cal's outstretched hand and hauled his younger brother to his feet.

Cal brushed at his clothes for a moment then adjusted the gun belt at his waist.

Trace handed him the revolver.

The chambers clicked ominously as Cal checked them before sliding the Colt back into the holster. "I know who did it. I smelled him right before he hit me."

"Bobcat?"

"Yep."

"Let's get back to Greeley's place and see if the good parson knows where we can find Bobcat." Trace almost smiled when Cal shook off his attempts to help him. "Fine, I won't nursemaid you, but don't ever scare me like that again. I thought you were dead."

"Right now, my head wishes I was."

Trace wished he didn't have to go back and face the accusations in Lily's eyes. He gripped his rifle and steeled himself for the ordeal, his muscles tightening with every step. And he never let up on his vigilance, keeping to the shadows and the shortest route to get Cal under cover.

Greeley opened the door to Trace's pounding. Puzzlement covered the parson's face, and he reached out to grab Cal and draw him inside.

"What happened?" Lily thrust the baby into the arms of the pastor's wife and rushed to Cal's side.

"Nothing to worry about, Lily." Cal tried to smile, wincing with the effort. "A crack to the head's all."

"It looks terrible. Does it hurt? Here, sit down." She pushed him toward a chair, turning his face to the lamplight to examine the injury.

Trace leaned his rifle against the wall by the door and crossed his arms.

Lily withdrew a handkerchief from her sleeve and dabbed at the blood oozing from Cal's temple, all the while keeping up a steady stream of sympathy.

Something twisted in Trace's gut. What would it be like to have Lily fuss over him like that? He squashed the thought down. He had to be all kinds of an imbecile to wish he could swap places with his little brother right now.

"What happened out there?" Greeley stoked the fire. Trace didn't miss the bulge of the gun under his coat. "Did you find out where they were heading?"

Lily's eyes searched out Trace, pinning him with their questions. Her hands gripped the cloth she'd been using on Cal and her bottom lip disappeared behind her teeth.

He hated to be the one to dash her hopes, but he wouldn't lie to her. "I'm sorry, Lily. I lost them. I don't know where they went."

NINE

This is what you get for relying on a man.

Silent tears tracked down Lily's cheeks. She turned away from Trace and dipped the corner of her cloth into the basin of water Pastor Greeley set at her elbow. With gentle strokes she cleaned the blood and dirt from the nasty swelling on Cal's temple. She avoided his eyes. The lump in her throat grew, and the walls of the cabin closed in. "You've got a goose egg, but I think the bleeding has stopped." Lily stepped back, folding the cloth. Her voice sounded as tight as it felt, thin and controlled. Her feelings hung on cobwebs, like if she moved too fast she'd jar everything loose.

Cal winked at her, his mouth quirking up in a smile. "Good thing I've got such a hard head. Thanks for taking care of me."

Greeley poured a cup of coffee and handed it to Cal. "One of the kidnappers hit you?"

"No." He sipped the brew, blinked, grimaced, and set the cup down. "It was Bobcat. I followed the kidnappers behind the hotel. They were heading toward the livery when he clobbered me."

The look on Greeley's face caused gooseflesh to skitter across Lily's skin. He contemplated his coffee.

Trace turned Cal's chin toward the light and examined the swelling on his temple. "Bobcat couldn't have passed on the word that we were the law or the kidnappers never would've agreed to meet with us."

"No, my guess is he's playing both ends against the middle. Or maybe the kidnappers told him to watch their backs until they were out of town." Greeley shook his big, balding head.

Trace's hands fisted at his sides, and his expression smoothed out. His steel gray eyes hardened. If Greeley's face had chilled Lily, Trace's froze her clean to the marrow. But his voice was calm and calculated. "Any idea where he might go?"

The pastor pursed his lips and rubbed the side of his face, his fingers tracing his scar. "I know where he's likely to be. He's sure to have gotten paid something by the kidnappers for setting up the meeting, and you paid him a little, too. Whenever he's got any money, he heads straight for an opium den down at the south end of town. Stay here with the ladies and your brother. I'll fetch him."

"Better if we both go. He might be trouble." Trace reached for his rifle.

"He won't be trouble for me." Greeley ground the words out, sounding unlike any preacher Lily had ever encountered. "Stay here." He checked his gun, reached up to a shelf beside the bedroom door, and took down a box of bullets, slipping them into his pocket. With a kiss for Mei Lin's cheek and a chuck under the chin for the baby girl, he settled his hat on his head and slipped out the door.

Mei Lin bowed slightly to Trace. "Do not worry about Hart. He will bring Bobcat back. As you may have guessed, he has not always been a preacher. Hart is able to take care of himself." She nodded toward the daybed under the front window. "Perhaps your brother would be more comfortable lying there." She shifted the baby, laying the child against her shoulder and smoothing the unruly baby hair. The infant relaxed against Mei Lin, stuck her thumb into her mouth, and closed her eyes. "When you are ready, Lily, you can sleep in my room. Hart will bed down out here." She looked from

Lily to Trace and back again.

Lily hadn't given a thought to the sleeping arrangements, being so focused on the fact that Rose was still in the hands of the kidnappers. Mei Lin closed the bedroom door behind her, leaving Lily alone with Cal and Trace.

"She's right, Cal." Trace motioned toward the bed. "You should get some rest. And you, too, Lily. I'll wait for Greeley to get back."

Lily shook her head. "I'm not going to bed until Pastor Greeley gets back. I can't sleep without at least knowing where Rose is." She swiped at her tears with the backs of her hands then twisted her fingers together at her waist.

Trace looked like he wanted to argue, but then he shrugged and leaned his rifle back against the wall. "Suit yourself, but it could be a long wait and you should be prepared that Bobcat might not know where the kidnappers went."

Cal stood up with a groan. He pinched the bridge of his nose, scrunching his eyes closed. "I'm going to sack out for a while. Wake me when they get back, right?" He stretched out on the bed, careful to keep his boots off the spread. His eyes closed and he sighed, relaxing at once. His chest rose and

109

fell, and his hand across his middle went limp.

Trace was another matter. He paced the distance between the stove and the bedroom door, his boots eating up the space.

Lily sagged into the chair Cal had vacated, her thoughts boiling like beans in a pot. Her tongue ached with all she wanted to say, all the frustration and disappointment. But she wouldn't give in to the urge. Trace had accused her more than once of not being able to hold her tongue. She'd show him.

"This whole thing is your fault." The words popped out, despite her resolution. Exasperated with herself, she bit her lip. She knew she was being unfair, but she wouldn't take the accusation back. Her hurt was all she had to hold on to.

He stopped pacing and stared at her. "How's that?"

"I should be holding Rose right now. You promised you'd get her back." A fresh stab of agony sliced through her chest. Her arms felt as empty as her heart. She wanted to lash out, to hurt someone, something, as much as she was hurting. And Trace was the easy, available target. "You promised Violet you'd find her baby. You promised me."

Trace scowled, his mustache dipping at

the ends. "I know it. You don't have to remind me. I'm doing the best I can."

"Maybe your best isn't good enough."

He blinked and took a step back.

Propelled by frustration and fear, her words tumbled out. "Maybe I should've waited for Marshal Maxwell. Why didn't you arrest those kidnappers when you had them in that hotel room? Why didn't you make sure they were bringing the right baby?"

He paled, his jaw going tight. His eyes reminded her of chips of ice. "You have a lot of experience being a lawman? Maybe you've forgotten just what's at stake here. I didn't arrest them in the hotel room because Rose isn't the only child they've taken. Are you so selfish that you'd risk the lives of other children just to get your one baby back? The moment they get wind the law's on their tails, they'll get rid of the evidence. They'll murder those kids and bury them where no one will ever find them. Is that what you want?"

Lily sprang from the chair. She couldn't sit still anymore. Every muscle screamed to be doing something, anything that would get her baby back. "I just want Rose. I need her. Can't you understand that? I'm her mother now. She's all I have in the world. I should've known better than to trust you. I should've known better than to trust *any* man." Sobs crowded her throat. Grief for her sister, worry for Rose, and vexation at putting herself in the position of having to rely on Trace ballooned in her, made all the worse by knowing she was being unreasonable.

But what did reason have to do with feelings? It didn't help that she had started to care for Trace, had allowed herself the tiniest hope that perhaps he was the one man who wouldn't let her down.

Her accusations wrapped around him like coils of barbed wire. She hadn't said anything he hadn't thought himself, but somehow it sounded worse coming from her. She didn't have to resort to blame; her tears had been enough to tear his guts out. He needed to get back onto a solid footing, let her know he was still in charge of the situation. "You're acting like a hysterical female."

A laugh hitched on a sob in her throat. "I have news for you, mister. I *am* a hysterical female." She gulped in air and scrubbed the dampness on her cheeks. "How do you expect me to act? Not everyone is as cold and calculating as you. You must have ice water in your veins. I bet you've never loved anyone in your life so bad you'd do anything to protect them. You couldn't ever care that deeply. You have no emotions, no feelings."

The coils tightened. She was dead wrong. He'd loved that much once. Not that the depth of his love had made any difference when his mother and sister lay dying of cholera, with only Alec and Cal and Trace to look on. Feelings couldn't be relied on in a pinch. Feelings were as useful as spitting into the wind when it came to getting a job done. He'd vowed never to let himself feel that deeply. "You don't know what you're talking about. If you weren't so wrapped up in your feelings and emotions that you can't think straight, maybe you'd remember that other families have lost their kids, too. Don't you think they want 'em back?"

He flung his hands up then shoved them in his pockets. "I never should've let you come. This investigation was doomed before it started, bringing a civilian — a *female* civilian — along. Come morning, you're going back to Money Creek." The moment the words left his lips, he regretted them. Hard as it was to admit, he'd grown used to her being with him. The thought of sending her back to Money Creek made his stomach clench.

She gasped, her mouth dropping open.

Her blue-green eyes disappeared behind her lids as she blinked long, grabbing the back of the chair to steady herself.

Guilt ripped through him. She was overwrought, and he was firing back at her because she'd hurt him. Just like his father, lashing out at those closest to him when their words hit too close to the mark. "Lily, I'm —"

Her hand shot out to halt him. "Don't." Her chin came up. "I don't know why I trusted you. I thought you were somebody special. I should've known better. You might be ready to abandon the investigation, to turn tail and run, but I'm not. I'm not going back to Money Creek without my niece. I don't need your help. I'll find Rose on my own."

"What makes you think I'm ready to run?" What kind of a man did she think he was? He might be like a calf in front of a cutting horse with this case, headed and barred from the direction he wanted to go, no matter which way he dodged, but he'd never turn yellow and run. "I never said that."

Her lips quivered for a second, making him feel like more of a heel than ever. "You said we were going back to Money Creek."

"You only hear what you want to hear.

114

Quit twisting my words. I said *you* were going back to Money Creek. I never said anything about me going back. Cal will take you on the stage in the morning. He'll see you safe back home. I'll find out from Bobcat where the kidnappers have taken the rest of the children and go after them myself. For once in your life, you're going to have to trust someone."

The idea that he'd duck out in the middle of a case — that she *thought* he would — stung like a slap. The more he considered it, the more it chafed. He crossed the room in two steps and grabbed her by the shoulders. "I made a promise, and I aim to keep it. I'm a man of my word, and don't you forget it." He gave her a quick shake.

She made him so angry he needed to put some distance between them before he did something really stupid — like give in to the temptation to kiss her. The scent of flowers drifted up from her hair. He snatched his hands away, realizing his mistake.

She lifted her eyes. Fresh tears hovered on her lashes, and deep in those mountain-lake depths, he caught a spark of hope, as if she wanted to believe his words but was afraid.

His resolve vamoosed quicker than an outlaw with a posse on his tail. His hands reached for her again, this time cupping her tearstained face in his palms. He swiped the wet tracks with his thumbs, marveling at her soft skin, so smooth and pale against his tanned, rough hands. As he lowered his head to hers, her eyelids fluttered closed, and her breath seared his skin. A sense of inevitability swept over him, and he acknowledged how long he'd hankered to do just this. "Lily." Her name rumbled from someplace deep in his chest, a whisper and a promise all at once, though he refused to examine what that promise might be.

In the instant before his lips claimed hers, the door crashed open and Bobcat lurched through, sprawling in an opium-soaked heap on the floor.

TEN

Lily sprang back from Trace's grasp, her face flaming, and prayed the floor would open right up and swallow her whole.

Cal sat up on the daybed in a fluid motion, swinging his legs down. His eyes showed no signs of sleepiness. He shot Lily a grin that only increased her embarrassment. Had he been awake the whole time? His wink and chuckle indicated he had.

Trace bent and grabbed Bobcat by the collar and hauled him to his feet. The scruffy little man wobbled and dangled from Trace's grip. Pupils dilated, eyes glassy, Bobcat emitted a musky, exotic odor along with the stench of unwashed male.

Lily covered her mouth and nose and backed away.

Pastor Greeley hooked his hat on the deer antlers on the wall and closed the door. "He was where I thought. Must've hustled right down there after clobbering Cal. Hope he hasn't soaked in so much of that poison that he won't be of any use to us. Nearly swallowed his tongue and the water pipe stem when I hauled him up off that opium couch." Greeley hooked a chair with his toe and dragged it close. "Put him here."

Trace dropped Bobcat into the chair and steadied him when he would've toppled over. Bobcat's head lolled as if his neck was made of wet flour sack. "Wake up." Trace shook him.

"Whayawan?" He slurred his words, his eyes focusing for a moment on Trace's face then going foggy again. He giggled, and his hands twitched, as if looking for something but not knowing what.

"I want to know where the kidnappers went. Where's Brady?" Trace spoke slowly but forcibly, as if willing Bobcat to understand and come across with the information. His face had settled into a cold mask that shook Lily with its intensity.

The edge of the daybed pressed against the backs of her legs, and she sank down on the lumpy mattress. Her hands tangled in the fringe of a crocheted shawl draped over the end of the bed, and she pulled it around her shoulders, more to ward off the thoughts crashing around in her head than any cold in the overheated cabin. How could Trace be so gentle, so near kissing her one moment, and so focused and cold the next? Had she dreamed it all?

"Gar—" Bobcat swiped the back of his hand under his nose. His head drooped until his chin was buried in his chest.

"What did he say?" Trace looked at Greeley, who shrugged. Cal stepped close, grabbed a handful of Bobcat's filthy hair, and shook him so hard his teeth must've rattled.

Lily winced, tunneling her fingers into the soft yarn of the shawl, and gripped her upper arms until they hurt.

"Bobcat! Pay attention." Cal pointed the grimy face toward Trace.

Greeley stepped forward, glaring down at the man in the chair. "Tell him what he wants to know, or you'll be sorry." He didn't say how Bobcat would be sorry, but Lily shivered at the pastor's tone of voice. If he preached with as much conviction as he threatened, he'd be hard to resist.

The McConnells and the pastor made such an imposing trio, Lily hoped they wouldn't scare Bobcat into a dead faint. She felt a little light-headed herself.

"Where was Brady going? Where are the rest of the children?" Trace asked.

Bobcat swatted ineffectively at Cal's grip

and blinked like an owl in the noonday sun. His enormous pupils zeroed in on Trace, and he appeared to be trying to concentrate. He smacked his lips and blinked again. "Brady . . . Brady went to see Miss Jenny." His shoulders rose disjointedly, as if any imbecile would know that.

Trace pounced with a keen ferocity that gave Lily faith that he really might be able to get something useful out of this drug-soaked turncoat. He gripped Bobcat's lapels and hauled him upright in the chair.

"Who's Miss Jenny?" His harsh, demanding expression was so different from the warm, tender look he'd worn when he held her close.

Lily shook her head. Better not to revisit that moment until she had time to really contemplate what had almost happened — and more important, how much she'd wanted it to happen. She pressed her lips hard together and focused on Bobcat once more.

Bobcat giggled. "Miss Jenny's in Garnett." He lifted his hand and beckoned Trace closer with a loose-wristed wave. "He always goes running to Miss Jenny. Can't stay away from her."

A spark of hope lit behind Lily's breastbone. A name and a location. Something to work with.

Trace let loose of Bobcat, and he sagged back into the chair.

Lily rose, too restless to sit still. The clock chimed twelve times. "What do we do now?"

Cal and Greeley lifted Bobcat by his armpits and dragged his limp frame to the daybed Lily had just vacated. None too gently, they flopped him down on his back.

Bobcat's mouth opened, and a gravelly snore filled the room.

Trace put his hand on Lily's shoulder.

The warmth of his touch sent a shock through her, and she jerked her gaze up to meet his.

"*We're* not going to do anything. You're going to go get some sleep, and in the morning, you and Cal are on the first stage back to Money Creek."

Any softening she might have felt toward the granite-tough sheriff hardened at his insistence she return home empty-handed. "I'm not going back to Money Creek. I'm going to Garnett to get Rose back." She spoke slowly so he wouldn't miss her point. She backed away from him, making sure her chin stayed up, and she didn't blink or break the stare. He wouldn't change her mind, no matter what he said.

Trace hooked his thumbs in his back

pockets and pressed his lips into a line until his mustache hid them. His eyes narrowed, and a muscle flexed in his jaw. "Lily" — his voice carried a warning — "I'm not taking you to Garnett. That's another day's ride from here, and if you think Jardin's a bad town, it isn't a marker to Garnett. It's too dangerous."

"I don't care about the danger. Rose is in Garnett, and that's where I'm going. I don't need your help, and I don't need your permission. If you won't let me go with you, I'll get there myself."

Cal shoved Bobcat, rolling him over to get him to stop snoring. "Trace, I'm not going to Money Creek in the morning either. These are some bad folks you're chasing, and there's no way I'll let you do it alone. Besides" — he flipped his hand toward Lily — "if you get the kids back, who's going to take care of them? I don't know anything about caring for babies, and the last time I checked, you don't either."

The bedroom door opened a few inches, and Mei Lin slipped through. Pastor Greeley held out his arm, curving it around her waist. The look they shared — tenderness, affection, concern — set up a fierce longing and loneliness in Lily.

Greeley smiled down on his wife. "Did we

wake you? How is the child?"

"I was not asleep, and the child is fine." A soft light shone from her eyes when she mentioned the baby girl. "I could not help but overhear that you are determined to go to Garnett?" She directed the question to Lily.

"Yes. I have to."

Concern lined Mei Lin's brow. "Though I understand your desire to find Rose, have you considered what going to Garnett with these men means?" She spread her hands out, palms up. "Garnett is a long ride from here. You will not arrive there until dark, even if you leave at first light, and there will be nowhere for you to stay unless you choose to camp out or go to the hotel in Garnett. Have you considered your reputation?"

Since Lily hadn't given any thought to the logistics, only to her goal of getting to Rose as soon as possible, Mei Lin's questions caught her off guard. She had no ready answer.

The pastor's little wife continued. "There is damage already, leaving town with a man you are not married to and staying away for several days. If it becomes necessary, my husband and I can speak for your stay here in Jardin, but if you venture out with the

McConnells to a place like Garnett for an overnight stay, your good name will be ruined." She turned to Trace. "I have seen by your actions that you are a protector by nature and that you care what happens to those in your charge. Have you considered not only the physical danger Lily will be in if you take her to Garnett but also the danger to her reputation and standing in the town where you live? Have you considered the damage such a thing could do?"

Clearly Trace had not. His gray eyes flicked between Mei Lin and Lily, and his brows came down in contemplation. "That settles it, then. I won't be a party to sullying your good name, Lily. You're going back to Money Creek, and that's all there is to it."

Her back stiffened. "That's not all there is to it. I don't care about my reputation. Rose needs me. I'd do anything to get her back."

Mei Lin ducked from under her husband's arm and came to clasp Lily's hand. "Please, consider what you are doing. I know what it is like to have a poor reputation. Hart rescued me from a brothel in San Francisco several years ago, but mud sticks. Once you have a name as a fallen woman, it will follow you for the rest of your life. Though I am clean and forgiven in the sight of God and my husband, others are not so forgiving. I do not want you to go through life as I do." Her desperation telegraphed itself in her tight grasp and the intensity in her dark eyes.

Lily glimpsed in her tortured expression some of the slurs and rude behavior she must've suffered for so long. More suffering than even Violet had endured as an unwed mother. But how could Lily turn back now? Rose needed her. Was she willing to suffer unkind words and thoughts if it meant Rose would be safe? Of course she was.

Cal tugged on his ear and cast a sizing-up look between Lily and Trace. The light of mischief glowed in his eyes. "You know, there's a quick solution to the problem."

"What's that?" Lily pounced on his words. Desperation not to be shoved out of this investigation when they were on the verge of finding her niece clawed up her chest. She'd seriously consider any avenue that would mean getting Rose.

"Well, seems to me, the best way to protect you all the way around would be if you and Trace were to get hitched." He shrugged. "Then there's no question about your reputation. You could go with us, and no one could raise an eyebrow."

Lily's mouth dropped open. The idea of her marrying at all, and marrying not just

125

anyone but someone like Trace McConnell? Preposterous. She didn't need any man, much less one as unfeeling and remote as the sheriff of Money Creek. But if she didn't marry him, she knew as sure as she was standing here he'd put her on the stage home and go to Garnett by himself. These tangled thoughts spun in her head.

She waited to hear Trace's refusal of the idea, knowing he had no more desire to marry her than she had to marry him. And yet . . . The sweet instant he'd held her seared her memory. The image of his face so close to hers, the security of being in his arms, and the strength of his embrace flashed through her mind. Disappointment surged back that she'd been denied his kiss. Lily shook her head to dislodge those thoughts and focused on Trace's face.

His reddened face. Could it be possible that the stoic lawman was actually embarrassed by his brother's suggestion? Indignation flared. She wouldn't be an embarrassment to any man.

Eleven

Trace was caught like a bee in a bottle. Every eye in the room, save the snoring prisoner's, bored into him. Marriage? To Lily Whitman? "Cal, I'd like a few words with you outside."

Cal sighed. "Fine, but keep in mind, I've been wounded. Don't go pounding on me too hard." He grinned and opened the door, stopping on the threshold and looking back over his shoulder toward Lily.

When Cal winked at her, Trace shoved him forward. "Out." Trace waited until he'd closed the door behind himself before rounding on Cal. "Are you out of your ever-loving mind? Bobcat must've hit you harder than I thought."

Cal leaned against the log wall of the cabin. The moon cast a mellow light and caused deep shadows, while the noise of the town rolled up the slope toward them. The church lay in darkness, its spire pointing toward the heavens. "Why're you so sore? I think it's a great idea."

"You're crazy." Trace paced the hard-packed path in front of the window. A square of lamplight lay like a saddle blanket on the ground. He stomped through it, pivoted, and turned back. "There's no way I will marry Lily Whitman, got it?"

"I've got it, and with all your shouting, I imagine most of the town got it." Cal eased down onto the woodpile and braced his hands on his knees. "But I don't think you're thinking this through."

"Marriage isn't in my future. Especially not marriage to that magpie in there. Trouble follows her closer than her own shadow. Anyway, I vowed a long time ago that I wouldn't marry. And you, of all people, should know why."

Cal frowned. "Why not? You're young, healthy, and you have a good job. No reason why you shouldn't take a wife."

"Have you forgotten who we are? McConnells, that's who. Right this minute our dear pa is sleeping off another bender in the Money Creek jail. And as much as his drunkenness embarrasses his sons, can you imagine the humiliation it would cause Ma if she was still alive? How do I know that same weakness won't come over me someday? There's no way I'd put a woman through what Ma had to endure."

"That doesn't stand to reason. You're no drunk. You've never even had so much as a beer at the Golden Slipper. You and me and Alec pledged to each other a long time ago we'd never touch the stuff. And speaking of Alec, he married Clara, and they're doing just fine. He hasn't crawled into a bottle. And you won't either. You're as likely to grow a second head as to become a drunk."

The long-held fear gripped Trace's gut. "I'm not risking it. It's too much of a responsibility, taking on a wife. I don't know how to be a husband. Pa sure didn't teach us. I'm not cut out for marriage and taking care of a wife."

Cal snorted and crossed his arms. "You're full of beans. All your life you've been taking care of people. Why else do you think you became a lawman? You take care of a whole town right now. You always did your best to take care of Ma and Priscilla. You're not even the oldest of us boys, and you're still trying to take care of Alec and me."

"And look how that turned out. Ma and Priscilla are dead, and you're a complete maverick."

Cal chuckled and nodded, then sobered. "Trace, you have to stop blaming yourself for everything. Our family didn't die of cholera because of something you did. And I'm a grown man who answers for his own behavior. We're brothers, so we'll always look out for each other, but you're not responsible for me. And you're not responsible for Pa either. Pa's weakness for liquor is just that. *His.* And because of his weakness and all the trouble it has caused us, you'll steer clear of falling into it. But don't get off the subject. This isn't about Pa and red-eye. It's about you marrying Lily."

Trace resumed his pacing. "I'm not marrying her. You're taking her home on the stage tomorrow morning."

"Well, I'm just not. Like I said, you're not responsible for me. I'm going to Garnett. And from the sounds of things, so is Lily. You heard what she said, and you heard what Mrs. Greeley said, too. You've already put Lily's reputation in jeopardy just by bringing her this far. And you know yourself how tricky a reputation is in Money Creek. Lily is as good as gold, but that won't matter to the biddies."

Guilt pressed down on Trace's shoulders. Why hadn't he thought of how it would look to bring Lily with him? What would happen among the good people of Money Creek when she returned? Would they shun her as they'd shunned the McConnells all their lives?

"And that isn't all." Cal touched the swelling on his temple. "There's the fact that you like her. I think you like her a lot, though you won't admit it. After all, awhile ago you came within a whisker of kissing her. You must feel something for her."

"Stop it." Trace contemplated the stars. "You're worse than an old woman."

"Face it, big brother — she's gotten to you. You care about her, and I think you have since she came to town. I'm not blind. How many pieces of pie did you eat at the Rusty Bucket before Lily took over the baking? And how many do you eat now? You're forever hoping she'll come out of the kitchen so you can see her."

"You're nuttier than a pecan tree. The whole town eats more pie at the Rusty Bucket since Lily came. She makes good pie. That doesn't mean they're all in love with her."

"The whole town doesn't stand in the jailhouse door waiting for a glimpse of her crossing the street. The whole town doesn't stop cold whenever they run into her because they can't get over how pretty her eyes are."

Trace halted. His mouth went dry. How

131

on earth did Cal know that? A lucky guess?

"I told you I wasn't blind. It's plain as a buffalo in a henhouse you're taken with her."

The truth rose up and smacked Trace in the head . . . and the heart. He did care for Lily. As much as she exasperated him, there was something about her that had burrowed into his soul. He shook his head. "I'm not saying you're right, but if you were, that would be all the more reason to stay away from her. She deserves better than someone like me." He had to slam the door on those feelings before he did something stupid.

Cal sighed again. "Well, if that's the way you want it, I guess I don't have much choice."

"What are you talking about?"

"One of us has to marry her. We brought her here, put her reputation in question, and now it's up to one of us to do the right thing. I figured since you care for her, it should be you, but if you're going to be stubborn about it, then I have to be the one. I'll have to marry her." He stood, squaring his shoulders and taking a deep breath as if bracing himself for a big task. "I'd best go tell her."

Trace's hand shot out and spun Cal around. "You'll do no such thing."

"Why do you care? Stop being such a dog in the manger. You don't want her for yourself, but you don't want anyone else to have her. Why not?"

"If you don't quit this, I'm going to bust you right in the mouth."

"Socking me won't change what needs to be done." Cal put his hand on the door latch. "If you won't do the right thing, then I will. What's it going to be?"

Trace stood rooted to the path, torn between what he wanted and what he feared. Lily needed him, but she deserved so much better than him. He could protect her by giving her his name, but by making her a McConnell, would he be exposing her to a bigger danger? Marrying her might solve a problem now, but what about the sack full of snakes it opened up later?

"Time's wasting, Trace. It's you or me."

No matter which way he turned, he was caught. But he knew what he had to do. He had to protect Lily now. He'd worry about later . . . later.

"Me."

Lily gnawed the side of her thumbnail, waiting for Trace to come back in and put an end to this farce. The idea of their marrying was ridiculous. Why would she even consider such a thing when all her life men had only let her down? She'd be forever waiting for him to break her heart, get tired of her, and throw her out. Better to be alone by choice than because she'd been abandoned.

And yet Trace had never given her the slightest indication that he would abandon her. In fact, when she suggested he might be thinking about it, he got mad. And, silly as it sounded, his anger had actually comforted her. He wouldn't give up searching for Rose. In spite of herself, she trusted him to keep his word to her. But that didn't mean she wanted to marry him.

The door opened and Trace entered. He stood in front of the fireplace, hands on hips, and glared at her. "Lily, we have to get married. It's the right thing to do."

Not that she was going to agree to this, but he didn't have to look like he'd just licked a toad. "Thank you, but I decline your noble gesture."

"I'm not asking. I'm telling. Either marry me, or you go home in the morning. I should've thought it through before bringing you, what you coming along would do to your reputation."

The fires of rebellion lit in her middle. "Trace McConnell, are you deaf? I'm not marrying you. I am going to Garnett in search of my niece. I don't need your permission, nor do I need your help. I certainly don't need you to marry me, regardless of what you think." She turned to the Greeleys. "It's sweet of you to be concerned about my reputation and my safety, but there's no need."

"I'm not being sweet." Trace scowled as if she'd insulted him. "I'm being practical. Now, choose. Marry me or go home."

"No."

"No to the marriage or no to going home?"

She ground her teeth. *Obtuse* didn't begin to describe Trace McConnell. "No to both." Her lips were so stiff, she thought they might break. But she was holding on to the very last shred of her control.

Trace threw up his hands in a gesture of frustrated surrender, and she almost wilted with relief. Then he walked to his saddlebags beside the door and withdrew a pair of handcuffs. "That's it, then. You give me no choice. Greeley, Cal's coming with me to Garnett. I'd be obliged if you'd transfer my prisoner back to Money Creek and turn her over to Marshall Maxwell. Tell him she hindered an officer of the law in the performance of his duty. Have him lock her up, and I'll see to her when I get back with the baby."

Lily scooted away from the manacles and the hard gleam in his eyes, but the table cut off her escape. Was he enjoying this? Of course he was, the lout. "You wouldn't dare arrest me."

"Oh, I'd dare, Lily Whitman. In fact, it would give me great pleasure to toss you into a cell. At least that way I'd know you were safe."

She appealed to Cal. "You wouldn't let him do that, would you?"

He shrugged, a smile tugging at his lips. "I've learned not to stand in his way once his mind is made up. And it's for the best, especially if you want any chance of going to Garnett with us."

They all ranged against her. Trace stepped close, and her knees wobbled for an instant.

She lowered her chin and stared at him out of the tops of her eyes, tucking her hands behind her back and out of shackle range.

He bent his head to whisper into her ear. "Don't fight me on this, Lily. It's for the best."

His deep voice rumbled against her skin, making it tingly and warm. She searched his eyes for any sign of compromise or doubt. "You're not going to give in on this, are you? You'll really make me marry you?" Her words came out in a cracked whisper.

"I won't make you, but I'm serious about sending you home if you don't. I couldn't live with myself if I caused any harm to your reputation. I've lived with folks thinking the worst of me all my life, and I'll do anything I can to protect you from that. I promised Violet I'd find her baby and that I'd look after you both. And there isn't just you and me to consider. Think about Rose. You might not care what the people of Money Creek say about you, but Rose will care someday. Folks might talk bad about her being raised by an aunt who'd run off for a while with a couple of men. I can protect you both from that."

His certainty wrapped around her like a warm blanket. She might not need his protection, but she had to admit she kind of liked it. And he had a point Lily hadn't considered before. What about Rose? Didn't she owe it to Rose to keep herself above suspicion as much as she was able?

But marriage? The thought terrified Lily. What if Trace walked away from her later? She bit her lip. The mention of his promise to Violet reminded her of her own. She'd asked God for help. Was this His way of

137

providing it?

The baby girl cried from the other room, and Mei Lin hurried in to check on her.

The sound of the sobs wrenched Lily's heart. Was Rose crying right now, alone and afraid? Her resolve to get to her niece strengthened and she straightened her spine. "If that's the way it has to be, then yes, I'll marry you, Trace McConnell."

Greeley grabbed up his Bible and motioned them into position before him as if he feared she might change her mind if he tarried. Cal stood beside Trace, and Mei Lin emerged from the bedroom, holding the little girl, and stood beside Lily.

As Trace began the familiar words of the vows, the enormity of what Lily was doing crashed over her. Trace's voice was deep and steady, as it always was. Did he have any idea what they were getting into?

Panic turned the uneasy feeling in her middle to a full-blown tempest when it came time to say her vows. Love, honor, and obey Trace McConnell, till death parted them?

Then he took her hand in his. His rough palm pressed against hers, and the strength that flowed from his fingers reassured her. He gave her hand a squeeze, and she stared into his eyes.

"I, Lily Whitman, take you, Trace McConnell, as my wedded husband, to have and to hold from this day forward, for better, for worse, for richer, for poorer, in sickness and in health, to love, honor, and obey until death do us part."

Or until you leave me.

She resolved to guard against any tender feelings toward Trace. Getting married for expediency's sake was one thing. Trusting a man with her heart was something altogether different.

"I now pronounce you man and wife. You may kiss the bride."

Lily blinked. She hadn't considered this part of the ceremony.

Trace must've forgotten it, too, because his Adam's apple lurched, and he dropped her hand like it was a hot stove lid. He rubbed his fingertips on his thighs.

"Well, go on, kiss her." Cal poked Trace in the back.

Trace swallowed again and cupped her shoulders. His mustache brushed her cheek just before his lips settled on hers, soft as a whisper.

When he lifted his head, she realized her folly in thinking she could protect her heart from him. He already had enough of that traitorous organ to break it into tiny pieces.

When he decided he was tired of her and abandoned her, she would have no defense against the pain of her loss.

She had fallen in love.

TWELVE

Marrying Trace McConnell was the dumbest thing she'd ever done. Sleep had eluded her completely last night. Lying in bed next to Mei Lin and the baby, she'd contemplated the ramifications of her decision and come to the conclusion that she was an idiot.

The sounds of Bobcat's snores and someone, probably Trace, pacing the floor provided background noise for her rampaging thoughts. Not exactly how she'd imagined spending a wedding night. Not that she'd imagined those sorts of things, since she'd never intended to marry.

Breakfast was a hurried affair at which she decided to ignore her new husband. Which wasn't as hard as she feared, because he wasn't in the cabin.

"The men went to get the horses from the livery." Mei Lin set a steaming cup of coffee on the table in front of Lily. "They will be back soon."

Trace stalked into the cabin and grabbed his saddlebags from the chair by the door. "Can you ride?"

She jumped when she realized Trace had actually deigned to speak to her. "Of course I can." Well, she supposed she could. How hard could it be? And if she even whispered that she hadn't been on a horse since a single pony ride as a child, Trace would have her handcuffed and on the Money Creek stage before she could say "sweet potato pie."

"Hurry up. Daylight's wasting." Trace headed out the door, his rifle resting on the saddlebags slung over his shoulder.

And good morning to you, too. Lily set her coffee cup on the table and stood. "Mei Lin, thank you for your hospitality."

Mei Lin looked up from spooning oatmeal into the baby's mouth and smiled. "It has been my pleasure, and you are welcome here anytime." She handed the little girl a crust of toast to gnaw on in her basket and wiped her hands on her apron before coming around the table to hug Lily. "Things will work out fine for you. We will be praying you find your niece safe and well. Trust God, Lily. He is in control, no matter how things appear right now. And trust Trace.

God brought him as a blessing into your life just when you needed him. Just like God brought Hart into my life."

Lily nodded, though she had to admit that at the moment Trace seemed more of a trial than a blessing.

Three horses stood saddled and waiting in front of the cabin. Lily paused in the doorway to inhale the misty morning air, cool enough to remind her that fall was fast approaching. The reason for this journey, always in the back of her mind, stampeded to the forefront. Was Rose warm enough? Did she have anything to eat? Had she already been sold to someone somewhere? Fear crawled up Lily's throat and lodged there.

"And they that know thy name will put their trust in thee, for thou, Lord, hast not forsaken them that seek thee."

The promise rose unbidden. And the truth of the verse hummed in her mind. God was faithful. He hadn't forsaken her, no matter how often life's blows came at her. All He asked was for her to trust. Such a simple word, yet so hard to do. Contrition swept through her. She hadn't even been trying to trust anyone but herself for a long time.

"And they that know thy name will put their trust in thee, for thou, Lord, hast not forsaken

them that seek thee."

A little of the tightness in her chest eased as she repeated the words. As hard as it was for her to let go of her doubts, to put her trust in anyone or anything besides herself, she knew this problem was bigger than her abilities. She needed God's help.

While Trace and Cal tied saddlebags and prepared to leave, she bowed her head and whispered a prayer. "Lord, I have to trust You, that You love Rose even more than I do. You know exactly where she is, and You are strong enough to protect her. Help me to find her, and help me know how to get along with Trace."

When she lifted her head, her heart, though still anxious, calmed a bit. She squared her shoulders, ready to find Rose, ready to make the best of her marriage to Trace, and most of all, ready to practice trusting God.

Cal smiled and motioned for her to come to him. "Got this mare from the livery this morning. The wrangler promised she wouldn't bite or buck."

Lily sidled up to the rangy brown horse. Couldn't they have found something smaller? "She'll do nicely." She tried to infuse her voice with more confidence than she felt. She gathered the reins and grabbed the saddle horn.

"Hang on." Cal winked at her and took her elbow. "Always mount on the near side."

"This is the side nearest me." She wrinkled her brow, trying to understand.

He blinked and cocked his head. "I mean you always mount from the left side of the horse."

"Why? The horse is just as high on both sides, isn't she?"

His lips twitched, and he pushed his hat back on his head and scratched his hairline. "Well, you just do. That's the way she's been trained. You did say you could ride, didn't you?"

"For Rose, I can do anything." Lily marched around the horse's rump to the left side.

Cal followed and took her elbow to help her mount, but before she could lift her foot to the impossibly high stirrup, Trace shouldered in. "I'll do it. She's my wife." The word "wife" sounded like he'd swallowed a fistful of gravel and got it stuck halfway down.

"I can do it myself." Lily scowled up at him.

"I don't doubt you'd get up there eventually, but I don't have all day." He put his hands on her waist and tossed her into the saddle.

As promised, the mare stood still, dozing in the sun while Lily adjusted her skirts to cover her legs. Her face burned, as did her temper at being heaved about like a sack of sugar.

Trace swung into his saddle and lifted the reins. He tipped his hat to Mei Lin and leaned out of the saddle to shake Greeley's hand. "Much obliged for all you've done."

"Godspeed, McConnell. We'll be praying. And I'll make sure Bobcat stays close, in case you want to find him again later."

Trace didn't spare Lily so much as a glance but lifted his reins and kicked his horse in the ribs.

Lily's horse, roused by the movement, started after him at an ambling walk. She grabbed the saddle horn and swayed on her perch. The long distance to the ground assured her that staying on was preferable by far to falling off. With fumbling fingers, she picked up the reins and tried to mimic the way Trace held his. She'd never be able to copy the easy way he rode, so instead she concentrated on just not falling off.

He kicked his horse again, and the animal picked up the pace.

Lily's mount followed suit and a horrible

146

jouncing began that threatened to jar Lily's teeth loose. Her backside slammed into the saddle again and again, and she began to slip to one side.

Just when she knew she was going over, Cal appeared on her right and grabbed her elbow, settling her back into the saddle. "Looks like she's got a rough trot. Kick her into a canter." He leaned over and slapped Lily's horse on the rump.

Lily lurched and suddenly the jolting transformed into a gentle rocking. Her chest loosened a notch and fresh air flowed in. It wasn't until that moment that she realized she'd been holding her breath. Wind rushed past her, and the rocks and scrub whipped by. A laugh surprised her, bubbling up and bursting out, and she grinned across at Cal.

He grinned back. "You're a natural, Lily." He pulled on his reins and took up his position behind her as the trail narrowed and began an upward climb. "Keep going. I'm right behind you." Cal's words comforted her. He was so easygoing and considerate.

Unlike his stubborn, hard-as-a-burnt-biscuit brother. She bored a hole into Trace's back with her glare. She'd show him she was up to this trip. Her determination hardened to granite. As she had promised herself and Cal — for Rose, she could do anything.

After only a few minutes, her legs quivered with the unfamiliar strain of staying on her horse. Her back stung, and she arched to ease the stiffness. Worry and lack of sleep sapped her stamina, made her eyes burn like someone had rubbed a handful of sand in them, and weakened her determination to the consistency of an egg white.

The horses galloped on for what seemed forever, their hoofbeats thundering in her ears and fading away into the sagebrush and junipers. A headache began behind her eyes and pounded along in perfect time. And Trace never once turned around to check on her.

Lily lived several agonizing lifetimes on the mare's back. She ached from head to heels, clinging to the saddle, staring stubbornly between her mount's ears. Her thoughts alternated between begging Trace to hurry the pace so she could get to Rose sooner and screaming at him to stop this torment and let her rest.

"How you making out?" Cal called ahead to her.

"Fine." She could only manage the one word without a sob.

They alternated between galloping and trotting for most of the morning. Up and down, the trail wound and wandered. The hilly terrain prevented them from traveling in anything resembling a straight line, though she guessed they were heading roughly north. She could hardly bear the thought of how much farther it might be and how long she might be clutching this saddle and praying for a release from her ordeal. She blinked back hot tears of exhaustion and hung on, concentrating on Rose.

Eventually, as they climbed, the scrub and juniper gave way to more trees. The sunlight changed from harsh rays to diffused spots drifting down between the needles of the pines. Their resin scent hung in the air. Pine straw muffled the sound of the horses' hooves.

Trace pulled his horse to a stop, and Lily gratefully did the same. The mare lowered her head to snatch a mouthful of some low bush along the path, and Lily had the alarming sensation that she might slide right down the horse's mane.

Cal stopped his horse alongside and reached for his canteen.

Trace took off his hat and swiped his brow with his forearm. He turned to Lily as if just remembering she was along for the journey.

If she wasn't so tired, she'd blister him. "How much farther to Garnett? We must be nearly there at this pace."

His eyebrows climbed toward his hat. "We're not even halfway."

"But" — she squinched her eyes shut and pinched the bridge of her nose — "you said it was a day's ride. Isn't it near noon?" She licked her dry lips and tried to swallow.

Scanning the surrounding trees, he unwrapped his canteen from his saddle and yanked out the stopper. He used his cuff to wipe off the opening and handed her the canteen. His rough-hewn gesture of kindness nearly undid her control. Maybe he wasn't the ogre she'd been painting him all morning. He cared enough to give her a drink of water.

The tepid liquid slid down her throat, refreshing her. Amazing how such a small thing could put her back into a better frame of mind. She smiled at him.

Trace hooked his leg over his saddle horn and rolled his neck. "It's about noon now, but I've been holding back the pace for you. We won't reach Garnett until well after dark at the rate we're going."

Any good his chivalrous gesture had accomplished evaporated. Lily wasn't sure if it was just tiredness or if she really did detect

150

a note of accusation and I-told-you-so in his voice. At this point she didn't care. She had to get off this horse and away from Trace before she disgraced herself by either throwing a fit of epic proportions or throwing herself into his arms and demanding that he comfort her. Her emotions had never been so off balance. One moment she had hope; the next she plunged into despair. Why was she so irrational?

She shoved the canteen back at him, ignoring the surprised look in his eyes. "I'll be back in a few moments." With all the dignity she could muster, she swung her leg over the back of the saddle. Unfortunately, she couldn't stifle the unladylike groan that shot out of her mouth.

"You don't want to get down right now." Trace took a swig from the canteen.

Hanging half off the towering beast, her stomach pressed into the saddle, she glared at him. "You couldn't possibly know what I want. You've ignored me all morning. I'm getting off this animal right now, and you aren't going to stop me."

Arrogant boss-cat. She had business of a private nature to take care of. He might be a wilderness-hardened lawman, but she was a lady, and as such, she was entitled to a little respect and priv—

Her feet hit the ground, and pain shot up her legs and back and exploded out the top of her head. She buckled into a heap on the trail, gasping and fighting tears.

Trace let out a sigh that could've felled a pine tree and swung off his horse. He knelt beside her and reached for her.

THIRTEEN

The moment he touched her, she started sobbing. He jerked his hand back. If he lived to be a hundred and thirty-nine years old, he'd never understand women, especially this woman. One minute she was smiling at him, the next looking like she was a hangman and his was the closest neck. How could holding back the pace in order to spare her possibly be considered an insult? It was plain as a pig in a parlor she could barely ride. He'd been doing his level best to look out for her.

She huddled on the ground, crying so hard her shoulders shook.

Trace looked up at his brother, who shrugged and shook his head as if to say, "She's your problem, not mine." Trace didn't miss the laughter in Cal's eyes. He only prayed that someday Cal ran into a woman who would tie him into knots as easily as Lily did Trace.

"I think I'll scout the trail ahead a piece." Cal lifted his reins and took off, leaving Trace alone with a distressed female. The coward.

"Lily?" He put his hand on her shoulder.

"Leave . . . me . . . alone." She sobbed out the words.

Something told him he'd be in more trouble if he did as she asked. He gathered her into his arms and began kneading the back of her neck. She tensed and pushed against him at first, but he ignored her struggles, and in a moment she began to relax. Her sobs quieted to hiccups, and she snuggled deeper into his arms. He rubbed the stiffness out of her shoulders and back, and she sighed, melting against him. He continued working out the kinks for quite a while.

"That some better?" If she'd have waited for him to help her get off her horse, he could've hung on to her to prop her up until the feeling came back into her legs and backside, but he didn't figure he should say so right now. He stopped kneading and decided to just enjoy the feel of her in his arms.

Eventually she pushed away and sat up. "Thank you."

He had to bend close to catch her whisper.

Fine wisps of chestnut hair curled around her face, and a delicate rose color tinted her cheeks. And those eyes. Every time she looked at him with those turquoise eyes, it was like getting gut-kicked. He reached out and swiped at the moist tear tracks on her cheeks, noticing the faint dusting of freckles across her nose.

If his life had depended on it, he didn't think he could have stopped himself. He leaned in — slow, to give her time to run if she had a mind to — and brushed his lips across hers. Soft and sweeter than her pecan pie. She sighed, her breath brushing his cheek, and he kissed her again, this time deeper, wrapping his arms around her and pulling her close. Her arms wove around his neck, and her fingers touched the hair at his nape. A shiver raced through him.

"Ahem." Cal cleared his throat.

Lily shot out of Trace's arms like a frightened quail.

He gritted his teeth and fisted his hands, counting to ten, gathering his scattered control.

Someday I'm going to kiss that woman without an audience and without a nosy little brother.

He rose and helped Lily to her feet.

She twisted her fingers together, staring

everywhere but at him. "I'll be back in a few minutes." She walked into the trees.

Trace stared after her, his heart hammering and his mind galloping like a wild horse penned up for the first time.

"Sorry to interrupt." Cal's grin declared him unrepentant. "When I left, she was mad at you. You sure work fast."

"Leave off, Cal."

"Well, there's no need to get sore. Nothing wrong with kissing her. She *is* your wife, you know."

He knew. His mind had centered on nothing else since the ceremony last night. Hours of pacing the floor, hours of riding, wondering if he'd made the right decision. It had felt right last night, and it had sure felt right when he had her in his arms just now. When he thought about it rationally, he knew he'd done what he had to do. He was protecting her reputation, a reputation he'd put in jeopardy by bringing her on this trip in the first place.

But it was more than that, a fact he'd wrestled with most of the night. He'd protested having to marry her, but did he really hate the idea that much? A part of him had wanted to marry her very much — a part of him that he'd squashed down deep from the moment he'd first seen her. Cal was right. He'd watched her around town, had gone into the Rusty Bucket far too often, hoping for a glimpse of her. He'd left extra coins for Georgia to pass along to the Whitman sisters, Lily in particular, just to help them out. And more than one miners' payday he'd stayed close to their place just to make sure no frisky powder monkey or rock driller caused trouble for either sister. He'd been looking out for her for a long time.

Could Cal be right that he was falling in love with Lily? The idea made Trace's collar tighten and his hands shake. No, he wouldn't be so foolish. Protect her, yes. Love her, no way. That would leave him too vulnerable. Suppose she up and died on him; if he loved her, he might never recover.

She reappeared, brushing her skirts and fiddling with her hair. "I'm ready, and please, don't feel you have to go slower for me. I want to get to Rose. I'll endure whatever I have to." She spoke to some area over his shoulder, not meeting his eyes.

He had to admire her determination, but her pale complexion, heavy-lidded eyes, and stooped shoulders belied her fighting spirit. Trace handed the mare's reins to Cal and took Lily's hand. "C'mon, then."

An arrow of puzzlement formed between

her brows, but she followed him to his horse. He mounted, slid back in the saddle, then leaned over and slipped his hands under her arms.

She squealed when he lifted her up and settled her on the saddle in front of him. "What are you doing?"

"We'll go faster if you ride with me." Someone had inserted an iron poker where her spine should be. His lips twitched.

After sobbing all over his shirtfront, now she held herself away from him like he was poison oak. She could change moods faster than a barn swallow chasing a mosquito.

She muttered something he couldn't catch, so he leaned forward and stuck his chin over her shoulder. "What was that?"

She jumped away from him, her hands gripping the saddle horn so hard he thought she might dent it. Her frown scorched him. "I said . . . I've made a decision."

But she didn't say what it was, instead giving Cal, who rode beside them, a pointed look.

He grinned, took the hint, and dropped back out of easy earshot.

"I've decided that we should set some boundaries for our relationship."

"Boundaries?" A quick swipe of his forearm shielded her from a low-hanging pine branch. She sure loved bossing him around. He could hardly wait to hear what law she was going to lay down now. His horse, a muscular bay, lurched up the incline and broke into the open.

Lily rocked in the saddle, bouncing off his chest and bolting upright again. "I don't think you should kiss me again."

Disappointment shot through him. Here he'd been plotting just how soon he could get another kiss from her. "Why not? You're my wife now." Strange how saying the words didn't make his flesh crawl like he'd antici-pated. "And if I remember correctly, you kissed me back. You didn't hate it, whatever you're trying to tell yourself now."

She shrugged. "Kissing is a distraction. We should concentrate on Rose. Getting her back is all that matters."

"A distraction? I hadn't thought of it that way." What would he give to be distracted like that again?

"I'm just saying that Rose should be our priority. We'll work out all the marriage is-sues after she's safe. Until then, I want you to keep your distance."

Though he couldn't do anything to battle her foolish notions, he decided to do some-thing about her rigid posture. Without warning, he kicked his horse into a gallop.

Lily squealed and grabbed his forearms. He tightened his hold around her and forced her back against his chest. She soon caught the rhythm of the horse's gait. A feeling of contentment wrapped around him when her head leaned back against his shoulder. In less than a mile, she relaxed into sleep.

Tendrils of her hair teased his cheek. He eased back the pace. They wouldn't really make better time riding double, for he couldn't push his horse that hard. But at least this way she'd get some rest. He chuckled. Wide awake and fighting, Lily didn't trust him as far as she could throw a cast-iron stove, but when he held her as she slept, she nestled against him like she was coming home.

Somewhere in that exasperating head of hers, even if she didn't know it yet, she had to trust him. Didn't she?

They reached Garnett just after dark, and not once did Lily stir in Trace's arms.

He pulled up on a rise to study the town. A typical mining town, half tents, half hastily-thrown-together wooden buildings. Saloons predominated with some stores, a barbershop and bathhouse, and a hotel scattered among them.

Trace brushed his chin on Lily's hair.

Some of the baby-fine strands clung to the whiskers he hadn't taken the time to shave this morning.

"She could sleep through a gunfight." Cal yawned and motioned toward Lily. "I'll head in and check out the hotel."

Raucous music spilled out of the nearest saloon, and men roamed the streets in search of a good time. "From the looks of this crowd, we'd best pray there's a room available."

While he waited for Cal's return, he watched the town, trying to get a feel for things. Lights blazed from windows and tent flaps. A smart lawman knew the lay of the land and tried to use it to his advantage.

He cast back to what day it was. First of September. No wonder the town was near bursting. Payday for the local miners. The bars and brothels would be overrun. Miners' payday was always the worst day of the month in Money Creek. He hoped his brother Alec could handle things at home.

Cal returned and handed Trace the hotel key. "Room 6. Last one they had. And the lobby is swarming with men. I scouted things out, and there's a back way inside. I'll show you then take the horses to the livery. They're about spent."

In the alley behind the hotel, Trace handed

Lily down to Cal and dismounted. Cal eased Lily back into Trace's arms and motioned to the back door. "In there, then a left up the stairs. Room's the second to last on the left. There's a bench at the end of the hall under the window. I'll set up down there and keep watch. I'll bring your gear and your rifle."

Trace nodded, grateful to have Cal along. "Be careful."

Cal brushed aside the words and gathered the reins, leading the horses into the darkness.

Trace took one more look over his shoulder, grappled with the doorknob, and let himself into the hotel. A lone wall sconce lit the back hallway, and true to Cal's words, a staircase ascended on the left.

Lily stirred, tucked her head tighter under his chin, and sighed. Her breath on his skin made his throat close. Her boundaries were in serious danger of being breeched.

Stop hanging about and get her under cover. You're acting like a lovesick dying duck.

He fumbled with the key then eased the flimsy door aside. The room was nothing to brag about. Moonlight filtered through the open window, and a breeze made the lace curtain belly out. Trace shut the door and leaned against it for a moment, glad to have

Lily safely inside. He took a deep breath, letting some of the tension of the day seep from his muscles. Drowsiness caught him by surprise, and he shook his head. Time to get Lily to bed. Cal would be back soon.

He stepped to the bed and lowered her to the quilt. She immediately curled onto her side and tucked her hands under her head on the pillow. He couldn't resist running the backs of his fingers down her sleep-flushed cheek. So soft and warm. She responded by curling into his touch and moving her lips ever so slightly as if whispering a secret. Trace pulled himself away. He checked the lock on the door then stood by the window, watching the town.

Several saloons occupied the opposite side of the street — the Blackbird, Rosie's, the Sluice Box, Miss Jenny's. The name of the next one was obscured in darkness, though he could see through the windows men drinking and playing cards. Coburn's —

His eyes swiveled back up the street . . . Miss Jenny's. His heart rate picked up. Bobcat had said that Brady always returned to Miss Jenny. Was it possible he meant the saloon and not a woman, as Trace had originally presumed? Or was Miss Jenny the name of the proprietress?

A tap at the door had him drawing his gun

as he turned. He glanced at the bed, but Lily slept on. He approached the door. "Who is it?"

"Cal."

Trace opened the door for his brother to ease through.

Cal let the saddlebags he carried slip off his shoulder onto the chair beside the door.

Trace took his rifle from his brother, glad once more to have it in his hands. Though he was fast enough with a handgun, he much preferred the feel and range of his rifle. "See anything?" Trace kept his voice low, though he had a feeling a city band could march through the hotel room playing "Battle Hymn of the Republic" and Lily wouldn't stir.

"Lotsa folks moving around. Miners mostly. Every last stall at the livery is full. Our horses are in a corral out back. I stopped at the desk and asked for a pot of coffee to be sent up. Could be a long night."

The coffee arrived as he spoke. Cal lifted the lid on the pot and the aroma hit Trace, making his stomach gurgle.

"I got some biscuits, too. Kitchen was closed, so this was all they had."

"Good thinking. And take a look at this." Trace grabbed one of the cold, hard lumps, probably leftovers from the morning, and motioned toward the window. "Check out the name of the saloon in the middle of the block. Miss Jenny's, just like Bobcat said." He bit down on the biscuit, grimacing as it crumbled to dry bits in his mouth. Too bad he wasn't at the Rusty Bucket right now enjoying some of Lily's light-as-air biscuits. He chuckled to himself. Maybe being married to Lily wouldn't be all bad. He already liked her cooking and missed it when he didn't get it.

Cal walked to the window, his boots making barely a sound on the hardwood floor. He lifted aside the curtain to peer out. "You want I should go down there and poke around? I don't think Brady would know me." Cal rested his hand on his gun butt and pursed his lips, surveying the scene.

"I'd rather you stood watch in the hallway, like we talked about. I don't fancy you walking into a saloon full of armed men when we don't know who all the bad guys are yet. And don't forget, if they get wind of us nosing around, they might just ditch the evidence." Trace's chest tightened at the thought. He glanced again at Lily, knowing he had to get this right or he'd never be able to keep the promises he'd made, never earn her trust. "Tomorrow will be soon enough. The town's not that big. If the kids are here, we should be able to get a line on where they are."

"Where're you going to start?"

"There." He motioned to the line of tents behind the saloons. "In the dovecote."

"Soiled doves aren't the most reliable source of information, are they?" Cal raised a single eyebrow.

Trace nodded, smoothing his mustache then scratching his cheek. "They can be. In Money Creek, if you want to know what's going on in town, you ask some of the girls at Mabel's or the Golden Slipper. Like as not, they know. If Brady's got the kids nearby, chances are good at least one of the saloon girls will have an idea where they might be."

"Chances are one of those girls will go right to Brady and tell him we're asking questions," Cal said.

"I know it. We'll have to be real careful. First light would be best, after business dies down but before they go to bed for the day."

Cal stretched, arching his back and reaching over his head. "Well, I'd best get out there on watch. If you need anything, let me know." He slipped out, his tread silent.

Trace washed down the biscuit with a cup of almost-hot coffee. Maybe he'd best cover Lily up. He walked to the bedside and took

166

the blanket from across the end of the bed. Shaking out the folds, he bent over her and draped the fabric. One corner bunched up, and he leaned down to straighten it.

As he did, her eyes flew open and she gasped. "What are you doing?" Her shriek nearly blew his hat off.

FOURTEEN

Lily clutched the blanket to her chest, scooting away from Trace's looming form. Panic grabbed her throat and sucked the air from her chest. Sleep fogged her brain. She blinked hard against the gritty feeling in her eyes and tried to catch her breath.

"I was just covering you up."

"Why? Where are we?" She took in her surroundings. A bed, a dresser, a washstand.

"We're in the hotel in Garnett. Will you keep your voice down?"

"Why are you in my room?" Her muscles screamed in protest, sore from unaccustomed hours in a saddle. She stifled a groan and glared at Trace.

"It's our room. And will you keep your voice down? Someone might bust in here thinking you were being attacked."

"Our room?" A thousand thoughts stampeded through her head, and she bounded out of the bed, tripping over the blanket but catching herself before she fell. "We might have the misfortune to be married, but I distinctly told you there would be boundaries in our relationship. I knew I couldn't trust you. You're just like every other man in my life."

His head snapped back as if she'd slapped him. Winter blew into his eyes and stayed there. His features hardened into a glacier.

She backed up as he advanced, fear bounding through her.

He towered over her, crowding her until her back pressed against the wall. "Everything . . ." His whisper grated against her skin. "*Everything* I've done on this entire trip has been to protect you and to get your niece back. And not just me. Right this minute, Cal's spending the night on a bench in the hall, just to make sure you're safe. What do you want from us? From me? I thought for a while that you were starting to trust me, but I see now that'll never happen. You don't know me at all if you could even imagine — I may be a lot of things, but I'd never —" His throat lurched, the cords standing out on his neck. Pain seeped out of his every word.

For a moment, Lily wondered if perhaps she *had* misjudged him. But she couldn't back down, not when the fears and experiences of a lifetime screamed warnings not to trust any man. She lifted her chin and challenged him with her glare.

He sagged and turned away. "You're a stubborn woman, Lily. If you can't trust me, then we have no future. I'll be outside, where I intend to spend the night on watch. The *whole* night." Without looking at her again, he picked up his rifle and stepped to the window. She gasped when he threw his leg over the sill and ducked under the sash, taking up a post on the balcony. He sat under the window, his rifle at the ready, and kept his face turned toward the street.

Her legs wobbled, and she tottered toward the bed. The springs creaked when she sagged onto the mattress, her mind reeling, her heart lodged in her throat.

What had she done? The horrible accusations she'd flung at him echoed in her ears. And the cold fury of his assessment of her squeezed her lungs.

Hot tears pricked her eyes and blurred her vision. An empty feeling began in her middle and expanded to fill her entire being. Alone. Alone with her fears and doubts, with her distrust and pain.

Forsaken.

The words of the psalm formed in her head, repeating their promise.

*"And they that know thy name will put their
trust in thee: for thou, Lord, hast not forsaken
them that seek thee."*

Was it just this morning that she'd prayed,
vowing to trust? And yet here she was again,
needing to learn the same lesson over again
in a whole new way.

She lay on her side and drew her knees up
toward her chest, trying to wrap her fears
tight around her in the hope that they would
somehow lessen her pain. Tears flowed
freely, clogging her throat and nose, leaking
from her eyes. For a long time she let them
rain down, loosening the tight places in her
chest, not trying to sort out the emotions
that prompted her sobs.

She'd ruined everything. Trace had only
been looking out for her, and she'd pushed
him away. In spite of her despicable behavior, he still sat beneath her window, guard-
ing her. She'd hurt him terribly, and why?
Because she was afraid.

Afraid to trust him.

Afraid he would leave her.

Afraid of the love she felt for him.

This realization broke down the walls
around her spirit, and she cried out to God.
*God, why? Why have You pushed and prod-
ded me into this situation where I have to trust
him? You know my fears. You know what the*

*men in my life have done. Why can't I love
Trace without trusting him?*

Even to her own ears it sounded silly.
Could there be love without trust? And even
if it were possible, was that the kind of marriage she wanted?

Lily, do you trust Me?

She shied away from the question, but it
wouldn't go away.

Lily, do you trust Me?

She warred with herself, knowing what
she needed to do but resisting, begging God
not to make her answer. Yet she knew the
truth of His Word. If she would trust Him,
He promised not to forsake her. And what
would she give to get rid of this feeling of
being all alone and forsaken?

At last she acquiesced to His will. Fresh
tears came with her surrender. *Lord, I trust
You. Please don't forsake me. I need You.*

She knew immediately what she had to
do.

But she didn't want to.

But she had to.

When she had cried it all out to the Lord,
begging His forgiveness and abandoning a
dozen excuses not to obey His prompting,
she crept to the window. "Trace?" She knelt
and crossed her arms on the sill.

He didn't answer her whispered plea.

The smell of wood smoke drifted up from the street, and someone on the hotel porch below laughed and lurched down the steps. He crossed the street and went into a saloon. The doors flapped behind him.

"Trace." His name stuck in her tear-thickened throat, and she swallowed. "I'm sorry."

She didn't know how to interpret his grunt. He didn't turn to her, but he didn't order her away either.

"I behaved shamefully. You were right. Everything you've done on this trip has been for my benefit." She gulped in a breath. "You've behaved like a gentleman in every way. I jumped to the wrong conclusion."

He sat with his back against the wall under the window and to Lily's right. Why wouldn't he look at her? Did he have any idea how difficult this was for her? Someone had lit a bonfire in the street below, and the light of the flames flickered off his profile and raced along the barrel of his rifle.

"I don't expect you to forgive me, but I wanted you to know I trust you." The words slipped out more easily than she'd expected. "I realized tonight that I wanted your presence, your attention. I wanted you to do things for me, help me get Rose back, but I wasn't willing to trust that you would and could do it, that you would put me ahead of yourself, that you wouldn't leave me. I wasn't willing to be that vulnerable because I knew how much it would hurt me if you walked away."

He flicked a glance at her, which she took as a hopeful sign. "You aren't like my pa or like Rose's father, who both threw off their responsibilities as soon as the going got hard. You're not like any man I've ever met. I'm sorry I judged you by their standard. You didn't deserve that."

Trace had an idea of what it cost her to lay her feelings out there like that. His mind had been reeling since she threw her accusations at him. Falsely charged again. The plight of a McConnell, it seemed. He thrust the self-indulgent thought aside. But none of the slanderous things the residents of Money Creek had gossiped about him and his family had hurt like Lily's allegations. He weighed her apology.

"Trace, won't you say something?" Tears hovered on her whispered plea.

He took a deep breath and tried to put himself in her place. A woman alone in the world, recently bereaved, her much-loved niece kidnapped, and now married to a man she barely knew. Dragged across miles of territory on horseback until she was dropping from exhaustion then suddenly awakened in a hotel room by a man looming over her. Under those circumstances, he might've lashed out, too. "It's fine, Lily."

"Is it really all right?"

"It's really all right. You go back to sleep. Things will look different in the morning."

"I won't be able to sleep, not with you sitting out there not looking at me. I need to know for sure you forgive me."

He went perfectly still. "I told you it was fine."

"Trace."

"Yep."

She didn't speak for the longest time. When he decided she wasn't going to say anything more, she whispered, "Would you kiss me good night?"

If she'd have asked him to crow like a rooster, he couldn't have been more surprised. Wary, tentative of crossing some line he wasn't sure of, he asked, "What about your boundaries?"

"Just a kiss. I'll know then that you've forgiven me."

He pretended to mull it over, when all he wanted to do was leap through the window and grab her up like she was the last flapjack on the platter. Slow as a stalking mountain lion, he eased up and entered the room, giving her plenty of time to reconsider her request.

She stood in the center of the room, her head bowed, shoulders sloped. Her fingers gripped each other so hard, he thought she might break one. He eased his rifle down and rested it against the wall then walked to stand before her. When she raised her tearstained face, all the sorrow and remorse in her eyes branded him like a hot running iron.

He cupped her shoulders and drew her close. "Lily, I forgive you. And I hope you'll forgive me for flying off the handle like I did. I want this marriage to work, for you, for me, and for Rose." He kissed her, firmly, so she'd know he meant it, but not so hard she'd panic. Then, before he forgot all his good intentions, he set her away from him. "You'd best get some more sleep. Tomorrow'll come soon enough."

She nodded, looking a bit dazed.

A smile tugged the corner of his mouth. It was a start. He climbed back out onto the balcony to take up the watch, but his thoughts were on her and their future the rest of the night.

Thank You, God, for baby steps. I'm trusting

You to show me the way we should go from here.

FIFTEEN

It was still dark when Lily's eyelids fluttered open. Her thoughts went immediately to Trace, and she swung her feet over the side of the bed and sat up. She turned, bracing her hands on the quilt.

Trace slipped through the window into the room.

Her cheeks heated upon seeing him after the kiss they'd shared the night before — the kiss she'd been bold enough to ask him for. She wasn't sure just where to look or what to think. She settled for running her fingers through her tangled curls, trying to bring a semblance of order to her messy hair. "Is it morning?" Even her voice sounded like it was blushing.

"Near about. Cal brought some breakfast. He's gone to fetch some fresh water."

Lily mustered her courage and grasped for a little nonchalance. She gave up trying to smooth her hair and shoved the tresses

178

over her shoulders. The bedsprings creaked when she rose.

Cal edged into the room carrying a pitcher and a towel. "Brought you some water." He flashed a smile. "You look all rested up and rarin' to go."

She couldn't help but respond to his open friendliness. "Good morning, and thank you." Cal had more than his fair share of charm. He always greeted her with a smile and a kind word, easygoing, as if life was a lark. Fun for a while, but Lily had to admit to herself that as a day-in, day-out companion, she much preferred Trace with his quiet, steady, trustworthy demeanor. Trace was certainly a case of still waters running deep. She knew that once he'd committed himself to a path, he wouldn't easily be swayed. Cal might drift on the surface of things like thistledown, but Trace was grounded deeper than an oak tree.

She splashed some water into the basin on the washstand and dipped the corner of the towel in it. As she washed her face, neck, and hands, she contemplated her reflection in the mirror. Her spirit felt lighter than it had in days. Though part of her still agonized over Rose, she reminded herself to turn back to God for reassurance, feeling

His presence wrap around her and comfort her.

Lord, help me to trust You. Help me to know You're here and that You haven't forsaken me. Thank You for Trace and Cal, and please protect Rose until we can get to her.

Cal stood at the window and watched the street below. "We should get moving. It'll be sunup soon. Best to ask our questions before daylight. Less chance of being seen that way."

"Soon. I want to talk to Lily." Trace's deep voice rumbled through the room.

She parted her hair into hanks and plaited it quickly. "I'm almost ready. Where are we going?" Lily looked from one man to the other in the mirror.

Trace flicked a glance at Cal, whose eyebrows climbed.

Cal let the curtains fall back to cover the window. "You want me to wait outside?"

"Naw, it won't take but a minute."

As Lily finished her ablutions, her stomach growled, reminding her she hadn't eaten since early yesterday.

Trace lifted the napkin covering the plate and poured her a cup of coffee. A wisp of steam curled over the brown liquid.

She sat down in the straight-backed chair beside the bureau.

"Lily, you're staying here. Cal and I will be back as soon as we know something." He handed her the cup.

She took it, fighting the rebellion flickering to life in her chest.

His eyes bored into hers, as if waiting to shoot down any protest or argument she might make.

She reminded herself that she trusted Trace. "Fine. Do you think you'll be gone long?"

Surprise sparked in his eyes, as if he'd been anticipating a fight. "Not long." He cradled his rifle, crossing his arms around the weapon and widening his stance.

She took a sip of the coffee and grimaced. A bite of biscuit helped mitigate the bitterness. She dabbed her lips with the napkin and waited for him to continue.

Trace took the coffee cup from her and poured her a glass of water instead. "I mean it, Lily. You stay right here. Under no circumstances are you to leave this room before I get back."

"All right. Can you tell me where you're going?" She had heard him clearly and responded clearly. He had no need to repeat himself.

"You can't follow us, you can't go snooping around on your own, and you aren't to

181

open this door to anyone."

Irritation eroded her resolve not to argue, and she worked hard to modulate her voice. "Trace, I know you're worried about my safety, and I know you like to cover every contingency, but if you'll notice, I am not arguing with you about staying in the room. I merely asked if you could tell me where you were going and if you would be gone long."

Cal chuckled. "I think I'll mosey down to the livery and check on the horses. You can meet me down there when you two are finished *not* having this fight." He closed the door behind himself.

Trace set his rifle down and blew out a long breath. "Cal tells me I act like a crazy old woman sometimes. My brother Alec says I get obsessed about planning. But I don't like surprises, and I don't want any misunderstandings. A plan is only as good as your preparation." He nodded, so certain of his philosophy she wanted to smile. "Cal and I are going to question some of the saloon girls in town about Brady and the missing kids. They usually know if anyone's doing something they shouldn't." He crossed the room and reached down to touch her cheek. He tucked a stray curl behind her ear and trailed the backs of his fingers across her skin, making her shiver. "I just need you to promise me you'll stay here where you're safe until I get back."

She rose, and in a move she wouldn't even have dreamed of last night but had been hoping for since awakening, she slid her arms around his waist and placed the side of her face against his chest.

His arms came around her, and he rested his chin on her hair. The steady beat of his heart comforted her.

She whispered into his shirtfront. "I promise. I won't leave the room. You've been after me hard to trust you. Now you're going to have to trust me to do as you ask."

He tucked his finger under her chin and raised her face.

She stared into his gray eyes, trying to read his thoughts and send him a reassurance that she meant what she said. How could a man who could be so exasperating sometimes appeal to her so very much? Lily had to shake her head at how much had changed in just a few days. Where once she wouldn't have trusted this man as far as she could throw his jailhouse, she now depended on him. Depended on him not just to get Rose back or to see to their protection and safety, but to guard her heart. Because as surely as she was standing here in his arms, she'd given him her love. And along with her heart came her trust.

She stroked his cheek, feeling the rough whiskers he hadn't shaved in a few days, reveling in the warmth of his embrace. The realization that she had fallen in love with him burst on her like a firework in the night sky.

The impact of this revelation increased tenfold when he lowered his lips to hers. His mustache brushed her skin, and his arms tightened around her in a way that made her heart race and her breath stop.

When at last he broke the kiss, he closed his eyes, resting his forehead against hers. "I can't ask you to give something I'm not willing to give myself. I trust you, Lily. Now, stay here." With one more quick, hard kiss, he snatched up his rifle and left.

Lily flopped back across the bed and sighed. She laid her hand against her middle to still the jumpy, flighty feeling there, but it did no good. With a rueful smile she sat up and rummaged in the saddlebag hanging from the footboard of the bed. Her fingers finally clasped the hairbrush. She loosened the hastily fashioned braid and with long strokes untangled her hair and put it up for the day. Once satisfied she had done all she could with her appearance, she returned the brush to the saddlebag Trace had designated as hers when they were packing early yesterday morning. The opposite bag held his things.

She drummed her fingers on her chin, curiosity worming through her. She chewed one side of her lip, wondering if she was trespassing, then took the plunge, unbuckling the saddlebag and dipping her hand inside.

An extra shirt. She held it up to herself and smiled. The sleeves extended several inches beyond her fingers and the hem hit her just above the knees. She was married to a man as tall as a Ponderosa pine.

Two boxes of ammunition, one for the rifle and one for the revolver. She laid those aside, sobered by the reality of their situation. She prayed he wouldn't need those bullets. Next, she pulled out a Bible. Worn black calfskin, onion paper with the gilt edging dulled from use. She opened the front page. The once-black ink had faded to brown, but the message was clear.

To my son Trace,
   May these words be a lamp to your feet and a light to your path.

Love,
Mama

A frayed piece of turquoise ribbon stuck out from between the pages — an odd thing for a man to have. To whom had it belonged? A sweetheart? Lily filed away the question to ask Trace later. She flipped to Psalm 9 and ran her finger down the page to read verse 10.

"And they that know thy name will put their trust in thee: for thou, Lord, hast not forsaken them that seek thee."

Seeing the words in black and white drove home the truth even more. She closed the Bible and tucked it under her chin as she contemplated the promise. Then she set the Bible down and tipped the nearly-empty saddlebag upside down.

His badge fell out into her hand. Heavier than she thought it would be, she turned it over. Sheriff of Money Creek — all the responsibility of the office lay in those words engraved on the silver star. Responsibility Trace took seriously. Lily repacked the saddlebag but held on to the badge, contemplating what it might mean to be not just the wife of Trace McConnell but the wife of a lawman. Would the people of Money Creek accept her in that role? And what about Trace's family? Cal seemed to like her well enough, but he liked everybody. What about Trace's brother Alec and Alec's wife, Clara? Then there was Trace's father, Gus, to consider as well. Lily squeezed the badge in her palm. So much had changed in her life in such a short span of time. She repeated the promise from Psalm 9 once more. She wasn't forsaken in this world, and she didn't have to face these battles alone. With God's help and Trace's, as soon as they got Rose back, things would be fine. She was sure of it.

She went to the window and scanned the street, hoping for a glimpse of Trace or Cal. She heard none of the bustling, raucous noise of last night. In fact, the town seemed half asleep in the midmorning sun. A few horses stood at the hitching rails napping until their owners came to claim them. One storekeeper swept the boardwalk in front of his shop. The town had the appearance of suffering from an overindulgence of drink, a condition no doubt shared by many of the revelers of last night.

A tap at the door made her turn around. Lily couldn't quell the smile that stretched her mouth. He'd come back. Hopefully with news of Rose.

A piece of paper shot under the door.

Lily stopped, instantly wary. But the lock on the door remained fastened. With a mouth suddenly gone dry, she picked up

187

the note. Her hands trembled even as her mind raced. Perhaps it was nothing. Perhaps Trace, facing a delay, had sent her a note.

IF YOU WANT THEM KIDS TO STAY ALIVE, MEET ME IN THE STAND OF TREES BEHIND THE LIVERY. COME QUIET AND KEEP YOUR MOUTH SHUT. YOU DON'T AND THEM BRATS WILL GET THE KNIFE, EVERY LAST ONE OF THEM. DON'T TELL NO ONE. AND BRING THIS NOTE WITH YOU. I'LL BE WATCHING. YOU HAVE TILL HALF PAST THE HOUR.

The numbing ice water of shock cascaded over her. She blinked and reread the note, then read it again. Each time, her heart sank further. Assuming the note was true, and she had to believe it was, what should she do?

Lily ran to the door but stopped before she opened it. Trace's words repeated in her head.

"You're not to open this door to anyone."

Instead, she pressed her ear to the wood. No sound from the hallway. Had the messenger left, or was he waiting to pounce on her the moment she turned the knob? Trace couldn't have anticipated this turn of events.

How long until half past? Lily had no timepiece of her own, and the hotel hadn't provided one in the room. She spun and hurried to the window, slinging the curtain aside and pressing her hand to the wavy glass, praying to find Trace heading toward the hotel. Only the empty street lay below.

She turned and sagged against the sash. "Lord, I don't know what to do. I promised Trace I would stay here. But if I don't go, Rose will die." Tears burned her eyes and the inside of her nose. What should she do?

She spread the paper she'd unknowingly crumpled and read the message again. This could well be a trap. Rose might already be dead. Her heart lurched. What would Trace do?

His badge lay on the bed where she'd left it. She lifted it, holding it against her heart. She knew what Trace would do. He would plan, and he would act. Rose's life was more important than any promise she'd made. Trace would never stay here in the hotel room waiting. Not after getting a message like this.

And with calming certainty, Lily knew that no matter what, Trace would come after her. He would find her. And she trusted it would be in time. She trusted him to be true to his calling as a lawman, and even more, she trusted the love she could feel growing between them, though Trace had never said the words aloud to her.

The note went into her pocket. How she wished she had a weapon of some sort, but she'd never fired a gun, and her only experience with knives was in the kitchen of the Rusty Bucket Café. What she wouldn't give to be in there right now with no bigger worry than if she'd made enough sour cream raisin pie to last through the dinner rush.

What message could she leave with Trace? She had no paper other than the note, nor did she have anything to write with. Conscious of time trickling away, she rifled through the saddlebag once more and pulled out the Bible. Opening to the inscription inside the front cover, she laid Trace's badge under the words and slipped the worn ribbon from between the pages and put it into her pocket with the paper. Then she slid open the box of rifle shells and scattered them onto the bureau top. Using the cartridges to build the letters, she spelled out the words TREES LIVERY ROSE. Her fingers shook, and she dropped several bullets onto the floor in her haste. It would have to be enough.

Her hand closed around the doorknob,

and she hesitated. This was her last chance to keep her promise to Trace and stay in the room, and yet she knew she couldn't. "Lord, help him to understand why I have to do this. And help him to find me quickly."

She turned the knob and peeked out into the deserted hallway. Tremors shook her legs, and she gripped the banister before descending to the lobby.

A green-visored clerk dozed at the front desk. The shade hanging in the front window slapped in a faint breeze.

Quietly, feeling eyes on her though she couldn't see anyone but the sleeping clerk, Lily passed through the wide-open door, hugging the front of the hotel and slipping into the alley.

She pressed her hand over the note, making the paper crackle in her pocket. The message said someone would be watching her. Was he looking now?

Sweeping the area with her gaze, mindful to check behind her, too, she edged around a slimy mud puddle behind the bathhouse next to the hotel, stepping over the channel leading from a drainpipe jutting out the back of the building. A manure pile rotted in the sunshine behind the livery stable. Air pressed in around her, but she couldn't seem to draw a decent breath. The stand of trees loomed ahead. Each step took her farther from the safety of the hotel room but maybe closer to Rose.

She stopped on the edge of the trees and knelt as if she had something in her shoe. Furtive looks over each shoulder showed no one. She withdrew the ribbon from her pocket and laid it on the path. A few quick folds to form the satin into an arrow pointing toward the trees.

Please, Lord, let Trace find it.

Pine resin aroma surrounded her the moment she stepped into the cooling shade. Dark branches, like heavily sleeved arms, hung down as if waiting to grasp her and hold her back. Gloomy shadows draped over her like a mourning shawl.

"Don't do nothing stupid now."

Lily froze at the sound of the husky voice.

"Almost thought you weren't coming." A man stepped onto the trail from behind a tree.

Recognition jarred her. She could almost hear the sound of the knife on the whetstone from the hotel in Jardin. A shiver rippled up her spine. She moved a half step to the side to block his view of the trail behind her, just in case he might be able to see the ribbon. "What do you want with me?" She forced the words past the lump in her throat.

"Plenty. Where's the note? Did you tell anyone?" He eased so close she could smell the tobacco plug stuck in his cheek.

Lily shook her head. "I didn't tell." She fished the note from her pocket and put it into his grubby hand.

"Just who are you people? It's plain you ain't no farmers looking to adopt a kid, not like you said you were in Jardin. Or are you mad because we gave you an Injun kid? I told Brady to give you the yellar-haired one, but he wanted to dump the Ute baby quick."

The yellow-haired one had to be Rose. Hope surged through Lily. "Where is this yellow-haired baby? Is she all right?"

"Special to you, is she? She your kid?" His gaze flicked over the paper once more before he shoved it into the pocket of his pants. Buckskin fringe swayed from his sleeves and shoulders, greasy and worn shiny. The smooth bone handle of his knife jutted from the sheath at his waist.

Lily didn't answer, afraid of giving him too much information.

"Them two men snooping around the soiled doves, they're asking a lot of questions. Who are they?"

Lily's mind scrambled for an answer. If this man knew the law was close, he might cut his losses and flee, but not before getting rid of the evidence. "They're my family." Just thinking of the McConnell brothers as her family gave her confidence. She was a McConnell now.

"Well, your *family*" — he sneered the word — "done asked the wrong gal. I saw the tall fellow with the mustache talking to Tilda. She has a big mouth. Stupid girl. I had to rough her up a bit, but she told me everything. Good thing I seen that tall fella on the balcony last night. I figured you was in that room. Knew it when they sent up breakfast for three. I probably should've tried to waylay them, but I didn't like the odds, not with the big fella toting that rifle like he knew how to use it."

A chill shot through Lily. She tried to swallow.

He must've seen her fear, for he cackled and spit into the bushes, gloating in the power he wielded.

She set her jaw and narrowed her eyes, shoving down her fear and letting anger rise. "Take me to the children." Never would she let this oleaginous snake make her cower.

He leered. "Oh, you'll see them soon enough. Get going. It ain't far." The sinister gleam in his eye threatened to erode her tiny courage. He spat a stream of tobacco juice into the undergrowth.

She forced herself to concentrate on Rose and clung to the promise that God was with her and the knowledge that Trace would find her before it was too late. What she had assumed was a small glade of trees was actually the edge of a forest that spread up and into a steep-walled canyon hidden from the town's view by the brow of a butte. The path, which she suspected was a game trail, wound through thickets and heavy growth that tugged at her skirts and hair. She lost track of their direction and with each step wondered if he was leading her so far from town to murder her and hide her body where no one would ever find her. But what else could she do but keep walking and praying?

After they'd gone what she figured must be at least three miles, though she couldn't be sure, the shadows thinned ahead. In a small opening in the trees, a dilapidated shack sagged among waist-high grasses. A piece of sacking wafted in the one window, and the door hung crookedly in the leaning frame.

"This is it."

Lily's heart raced. Either Rose was inside waiting for her, or this would be the place where Lily would meet her Maker.

Her captor sauntered past her and rapped on the door with the handle of his knife. "Wanda, we're coming in." He wrenched the protesting door open and motioned for Lily to enter.

She clenched her fists and steeled her resolve, though everything in her wanted to run.

Mr. Knife grabbed her upper arm and forced her into the room. "You behave yourself, or I'll kill them kids."

A filthy stench assaulted her the moment she stepped into the gloom. Unwashed bodies, moldering food, and rotting wood — the odors hung like a miasma in the air. She clapped her hand over her nose and mouth as she adjusted to the gloom.

Several pairs of eyes stared at her out of dirty faces. Children squatted and huddled along the back wall of the cabin. A table listed along the right-hand wall, and a woman sat beside it, half-sprawled on the rickety surface. An empty bottle of whiskey lay on its side in front of her outstretched arms. Her snores ricocheted off the walls.

Lily peered at the children, searching. It took her a moment to realize the smallest urchin was in fact sweet Rose. She was sleeping, her head on the narrow shoulder of a girl of about eight whose skinny arms clasped Rose as if to protect her. Tears burned Lily's eyes at the haunted look on the girl's face.

"Wanda, where's Brady?" The man kicked the woman's chair, jolting her out of her slumber.

She lurched upright, blinking and smacking her lips. "Hack?" Her frizzy hair obscured half her face, and she shoved it back. She scratched her side and yawned.

"Yeah, it's Hack. Who'd you expect? President Arthur? Now, where's Brady?"

"He's sleeping in there." She dug at her armpit, bleary-eyed, and poked a thumb toward a door on the back wall of the cabin. "What'd you think? That he'd be lolling around out here with these miserable brats? He staggered in around dawn and left me to watch the little beasts. And you, too, living it up in the saloon all night while I'm stuck out here." To Lily's ears, and judging from Hack's expression, it must've been an oft-repeated lament.

He picked up the bottle and inverted it. A few drops plopped onto the floor. "You're supposed to be watching these kids, not getting drunk, you boozer. What if one of them decided to run off? Brady'd have your gizzard served up with onions."

"They ain't going nowhere. Take a look at

them." Wanda suddenly seemed to realize Lily was there and blinked, focusing her stare.

Lily shuddered at the malice in the woman's eyes.

"What do you mean bringing a woman out here? Brady ain't gonna like that. You know what he said when he caught you sneaking Tilda in here last month."

"Shut up. We got trouble. I'll get Brady, but we gotta get out of here. This gal and a couple of men rode in last night and started asking questions this morning. Tilda blabbed everything she knew." He wiped his knife blade on his indescribably filthy pants and tucked it into the sheath once more. "She won't blab anything for a while now though."

Lily sidled closer to the children, wanting to snatch Rose up and hold her close, and kept an eye on Hack and Wanda. Then she realized the children were tethered together like a string of pack mules. A boy of about ten, the girl holding Rose, and another girl of about six were bound at the wrists and ankles; another rope joined them together and was fastened to a metal ring high up on the wall. Lily shook with anger at this beastly treatment. As if it wasn't bad enough to steal them and leave them in squalor.

Fury burned her eyes and throat. She whirled on her heel. "What kind of miserable humans are you, to treat children this way? Release them immediately."

The man grinned. "You ain't exactly in a position to order me around, are you?" He shoved her hard.

She slammed into the wall and lost her balance, sliding down with a bump next to the children. Her shoulder throbbed and her head rang. Before she could compose herself, her wrists and ankles were bound just like the children's.

"That'll hold you for now. Brady can decide what to do with you." He kicked her foot. "It smells like an outhouse in here. Stinkin' kids. I'm going to quit this racket and go back to robbing stages." He stalked over and banged on the door set in the back wall.

"Brady! Wake up. We got trouble." Hack turned the knob and slipped through the doorway. Thumps and a moan, and Hack emerged. Brady, looking less like an undertaker and more like an undertaker's customer, lurched into the room. Hack launched into a retelling of events while Brady held his head with one hand and the doorjamb with the other.

Lily sensed clarity of mind coming back

to Brady the longer Hack talked. By the time Hack had finished, Brady stood upright, his mouth in a firm line. He smoothed his fingers through his pale hair and adjusted his rumpled collar and lapels. "We'll have to pack up, then. Good idea bringing the woman. Another hostage might be useful." His deep voice again surprised Lily, so smooth and cultured in the midst of this messy cabin. "Get the wagon, Hack. Wanda, gather whatever wits and provisions you have. We're leaving."

Hack spat on the floor near Lily's feet.

She yanked her toes back and glared up at him as he laughed.

"It'll take me awhile to get the wagon here. I hid it more than half a mile up the ravine."

Brady nodded and disappeared into the back room once more. Hack walked outside, leaving the door open behind him.

Wanda staggered upright and headed toward the doorway where Brady had disappeared. "Wait. What're you figuring to do with the woman? I ain't watching her. I ain't being paid enough as it is." She ducked into the room, still scratching and complaining.

Lily tugged at the ropes on her wrists, but they wouldn't budge. She turned to the little girl holding Rose. Her voice snagged in her throat, and she could only rasp out a whisper. "Please, can I have her? She's my niece."

Rose, still wearing the gown Lily had put on her days ago, whimpered and squirmed.

"You're her kin?" The girl lowered her chin and stared at Lily out of the tops of her eyes, her expression doubtful. She kept her arms tight around Rose.

"She was stolen from me."

The boy rubbed his dirty hand under his nose. "We was all stolen." He stared at his bare brown toes then flicked a glance at her. "Are you here to help us?"

Lily could almost taste their fear. The tiny spark of hope in their eyes broke her heart. "I'm sure going to try." She spoke firmly, trying to make herself believe the words. Though now that she'd been tied, she didn't know how much help she would be. Still, being here, seeing Rose with her own eyes, was better than fretting away in that hotel room wondering. And Trace would come. He would find her message, he would search for her and find the ribbon, and he would help them all.

Rose stirred and opened her eyes. She stared at Lily. Dirt streaked her face, and tear-tracks through that dirt broke Lily's heart. How much had the baby cried since being taken? Then, like the sun coming out, Rose's little face split into a grin of recognition, and she leaned over, arms outstretched.

Lily lifted her arms and circled the baby, hating that she couldn't lift Rose properly because of the ropes binding her wrists. She used her elbows and inner arms to draw Rose toward her lap. When Rose leaned forward and snuggled into Lily's chest, Lily hugged the dirty baby to her, crying, reveling in the feel of the solid little body in her arms. "Thank You, Lord." Rose burrowed close, and Lily thought she'd never felt better.

Now all she had to do was pray that Trace found the clue she'd left him. And keep the children safe until he could find them.

Sixteen

Realization hit Trace like a punch in the gut. "What do you mean she's not here?"

Cal shrugged, and with a your-guess-is-as-good-as-mine shake of his head, he spread his hands. "I mean she's not here. Check for yourself."

He stepped back as Trace shouldered past him into the room. Empty.

She'd promised. From her own sweet lips, she'd promised to stay here in this room until he got back.

Disbelief made him go so far as to look under the bed, though he knew it was ridiculous.

"No sign of a struggle. Looks like she walked out on her own." Cal checked the street below, holding the curtain aside with the barrel of his rifle. "Maybe she had to . . . you know." He jerked his head toward the rear of the building. "I'll go down and check." Cal headed down the hall, his boots thumping on the bare boards.

Then Trace spied the pile in the center of the quilt. His Bible lay open, with his badge set inside the cover. A chill skittered up the back of his neck. In his heart he knew she wasn't out using the privy. She'd left the premises. Why would she leave when she'd promised him she'd stay put? Anger stiffened his muscles. She'd given him her word. She'd looked up at him with those amazing turquoise eyes and lied right to his face. Bitterness coated his mouth. His own wife didn't trust him enough to wait for him when she'd promised she would.

He turned and spied the bullets on the bureau. TREES LIVERY ROSE. His mouth went dry. How did she know? It had taken him and Cal several tries before they found one of the saloon girls who had the information they were looking for and who was willing to talk. If it wasn't for Tilda, who opened up like a creek in a flash flood, he'd never have known about the cabin in the ravine behind the livery stable. He wished now he hadn't taken the time to go into the Miss Jenny looking for Brady. If he hadn't wasted those precious minutes, he might've been back here before Lily took off. How long had she been gone?

Cal returned, pushing his hat back on his

head. "No sign of her out back." He hooked his rifle in his arm and planted his hands on his waist. "You find anything?"

"Just this." He motioned to the bureau and the bed. "The minute I turn my back, she takes off on her own. How on earth did she learn anything about that cabin in the trees behind the livery from up here?"

His brother studied the pile of possessions, his head cocked. Cal rubbed the hair under his hatband and resettled his Stetson. "Bible, badge, and bullets. Sums you up rather nicely. She's a smart little thing. She's trying to tell you something."

"Her not being here tells me plenty." Trace swept a handful of the cartridges off the dresser top and into his fist and shoved them into his pocket, then pitched the rest into his saddlebag. "It tells me that however she figured things out, she didn't trust me enough to keep her promise to wait here for me to get back. She's going to try to rescue Rose without any help, and she's walking into danger." He closed the Bible and yanked up the flopping saddlebag to stow his possessions. He stopped. The ribbon. Where was his mama's hair ribbon?

He scanned the bedspread, assuming it had fallen out of the Bible onto the crazy quilt. Nothing. It had been in his Bible when he packed it the night before they left Money Creek. He flipped through the pages and turned the book over and shook it. What had she done with it? He didn't have time for this. He had to get to her before Brady did. Wrapping the Bible in his spare shirt, he shoved it into the saddlebag and jerked the buckles. His rifle stood where he'd propped it at the foot of the bed, and he picked it up while slinging the saddlebags over his shoulder. When he caught up with Lily, he'd have a few things to say. "Let's go."

For once Cal held his tongue, and they exited the hotel, leaving a blinking desk clerk scrabbling for the key Cal had tossed in his lap as they walked by.

Trace swept the area with his gaze, hoping for sight of Lily. *Lord, she's walking into a snake pit and probably doesn't even know it. Please watch out for her.*

Wiping the sweat from his palm, he transferred his rifle to his other hand to repeat the gesture. He'd chased outlaws, rousted drunks — his own father included — and stood up to disgruntled miners intent on trashing Money Creek, and never in all that time had he been afraid. And he wasn't afraid now, he told himself. At least not for his own safety. But Lily. He had to protect her. She needed him, even if, in her I-can-do-it-myself-I-don't-need-any-man stubbornness, she thought otherwise.

Trace had to admit to himself that it wasn't her stubbornness that wounded him but rather that she'd broken her word. She'd seemed so sincere last night, shedding tears, asking for his forgiveness. And this morning, acting so calm when he told her to stay put, edging into his arms and hugging him, looking up with those amazing eyes, making him believe in the trust he thought he saw shining there. And the whole time she'd been lying, playing him for a fool. The realization burned like a coal in his chest.

They skirted the livery stable and stopped at the corner. The stand of trees Tilda had directed them to marched out of the mouth of the ravine a half dozen rods away. If they could trust the lady of the evening, Brady had a two-room shack in a glade up there. It was the only place he could've stashed the children. That is if he still had them.

Trace surveyed the terrain and weighed his options. Rough terrain and lousy options. "Get the horses and meet me in those trees. I'll go ahead on foot and see if I can pick up a trail."

Cal nodded, his light eyes never staying

still as he studied the tree line. "Watch out. They might have someone waiting to ambush you."

He flicked a glance at Cal. Trace wouldn't have wanted anyone else with him at that moment. For all his easygoing manner, Cal was as tough as a bull buffalo and as focused as a wolf on the scent when he needed to be. Trace needed him to be that tough and focused now. Lily had proven to him all over again that he couldn't trust anyone but his family.

Except that Lily was his family now.

They separated, Trace heading along the fence and Cal to saddle their horses. Trace broke into a jog, heading toward the trees at a crouch and half expecting to hear the crack of gunfire. He heard nothing but the sound of his footsteps and the thudding of his heart in his ears. Something caught his eye as he approached the edge of the pines.

The sun glinted off pure turquoise. He recognized the object right away. His mama's hair ribbon, one end folded to look like an arrow, lay in the dust of a game trail. The arrow pointed into the trees. Lily. He snatched up the ribbon and ducked into the undergrowth.

Air rushed into his lungs in great gulps, and he squatted, blowing hard. He didn't know whether to be angry or grateful to know they were on the right trail. The satin ribbon slid when he rubbed his thumb along its smooth, familiar length. He folded it carefully and tucked it into his shirt pocket.

A low rumble caught his attention as he waited for Cal to join him. A cool puff of air stirred the leaves around him and brushed against his cheek. Scanning the sky over the tops of the buildings, Trace scowled. A low line of angry gray clouds loomed to the northwest. He turned his back on the town and headed along the trail.

He hadn't gotten very far before Cal caught up with him, leading the horses. "Weather moving in."

"Yep."

"Gonna make tracking harder." Cal handed the reins of Trace's horse across to him.

Trace didn't respond. It didn't matter how hard the tracking would be. He wouldn't stop. They fell into single file on the narrow path. How far ahead of them was Lily? And what did she plan to do when she got to the cabin? If she got within earshot, she'd probably try to talk Brady to death, and he'd shoot her just to get her to be quiet.

The trail wound up into a deep ravine,

just like the saloon girl had said. A good hiding place, close to the town but isolated. If Lily had any sense, she'd just watch from the trees and not try anything heroic. But Lily didn't have any sense or she'd have stayed in the hotel room where she belonged.

Wind stirred the treetops, mirroring the gusts of anger and anxiety blowing through Trace. No doubt about it. A storm was coming.

SEVENTEEN

Wanda's haranguing went on, scouring Lily's ears, even through the closed door to the back room.

She glanced out the window, noting how dark it had become. Swollen gray clouds scudded across the bit of sky she could see around the dirty sacking. Lightning illuminated the air as the storm built. Brady's low voice rumbled, though Lily couldn't make out the words. The bonds on her wrists were so tight, her hands started to tingle.

Lord, how can I protect these children if I'm bound hand and foot?

She struggled against the bonds, but they wouldn't budge. "Can you help me?" She turned to the older girl, holding out her wrists.

"Nuh-uh." The girl shook her head. "Another boy tried that, and Hack hit him so hard it broke the boy's arm. He said if any of us tried it again, he'd break worse'n that. And that boy ain't here no more."

Lily's heart ached for these children. Kidnapped, abused, and terrorized for so long, they were now completely cowed and resigned to their fate.

Rose's body went limp as she succumbed to sleep, her breath light against Lily's neck. At least she was too young to understand most of what was happening.

Brady stalked through the room with a pair of saddlebags slung over his shoulder, Wanda scuttling after him, arms flapping and hair a grizzled, unkempt mass.

"I tell you, I ain't being paid enough to watch these kids and a woman, too. You get rid of her. She won't be nothing but trouble anyway." Wanda glared at Lily then back at Brady.

Brady laid the saddlebags on the table and turned, his ghostly skin seeming to glow in the gloom of the dingy cabin.

Lily's arms tightened around Rose, and the children crowded closer to her. His eyes reminded her of a trout's, glistening and unmoving.

Wanda jammed her hands on her wide hips. Spit glistened on her lips, and hectic color suffused her face. "You don't need two grown women here. If she's staying, then she kin look after the brats. I ain't going to do it anymore. You've never been grateful for my services. All you do is load me down with more work. Well, this is the last of it. I'm not going to take it anymo—"

Like a striking snake, Brady's hand shot out holding his revolver. Lily's scream collided with the gunshot. She had no time to cover her eyes or those of the children. Wanda's body rocked back and her face went slack, eyes wide and unblinking. Her thick arms flailed, windmilling to catch herself, but her heavy body crashed against the edge of the table, breaking it, then crumpled to the floor. As the thud reverberated on the heels of the gunshot, a tin cup teetered on the windowsill and toppled, clanking to the floor.

Rose, jolted from her nap by the gunfire, began to cry. Lily wanted to join in, but her insides were frozen. Numbness invaded her mind and body at the murder of an unarmed woman. She couldn't stop staring at the body just inches from her toes. If Brady would gun down his accomplice with such disregard and economy, what hope did she and the children have?

A wisp of blue-gray smoke curled from the barrel of the gun, and behind it, Brady's pale eyes gleamed, full of icy deadness. His face showed neither anger nor regret. He might have shot a rattler or a skunk instead of a woman. He turned to face Lily, his gun barrel swinging around and looming like a cannon's maw before her vision. "I can't abide a blathering nag. Wanda had one thing right though. There is no need for two women. You'll tend to the children." Again, his even, melodic tone, more suited to a poet than an outlaw, surprised Lily. He holstered the gun and picked up the saddle-bags.

You are not forsaken. God is with you, and Trace is coming. She repeated the promise to herself, forcing herself to believe its truth.

She tried to pat Rose on the back with her bound hands. Her throat constricted so hard she couldn't even muster a "shhh" to soothe the baby.

"He kilt her." The little boy gripped Lily's arm hard and whispered again. "He kilt her dead."

Thunder boomed and the clouds let down their rain, drops pattering on the dirt floor through the holes in the shake-shingle roof. Muddy puddles formed in an instant.

Brady looked out the door and brushed his sleeves. He shrugged his shoulders inside his jacket and smoothed his lapels. Long, cadaverous fingers brushed his thin hair.

"Hack's here with the wagon."

The clatter of wheels and hooves met Lily's ears. Where were they being taken? Would Trace be able to follow?

Hack met Brady in the doorway, water streaming off his hat. "Heard a gunshot. What happened?" He peered around Brady into the cabin. His eyes narrowed then widened when he saw Wanda.

Brady shrugged and ducked to peer out the front door at the leaden sky. "I decided she was surplus to requirements."

A gust of cool, damp air crowded through the doorway behind Hack. He stared at Wanda's body for a long moment then spit. "Toad strangler of a rain." His casual dismissal of the murder outraged and chilled Lily. She could look for no help from that quarter against Brady.

"Let's get rolling, then. If the weather hampers us, it will hamper those following us."

Hack stepped close and slashed the rope joining the three children together. Then he snatched up the boy under one arm and the younger girl under the other, and stomped out. Brady took the bigger girl and his saddlebags, leaving Lily alone in the cabin with Rose. But not for long.

"Gimme that kid." Hack reached down

215

for Rose, who still sobbed against Lily's neck. Lily jerked away from Hack, loath to release the baby. His hand flashed out and smacked Lily's temple, knocking her head into the wall. White stars burst through her vision, and her senses reeled. He snatched Rose from her arms, snarling. "Give us any trouble, and you'll wind up like Wanda."

Brady entered again. "Cut the ropes."

Hack's eyebrows rose. "What?"

"She's going to drive the wagon. If we're being followed, I want her up where I can keep a gun on her."

A stream of tobacco juice shot out of Hack's mouth, and he shoved Rose into Brady's arms before yanking the bone-handled knife from its sheath at his waist. Lily averted her face, not wanting to see the fatal blow, should he decide to use it for something other than to release her bonds. He cackled, clearly enjoying his power over her. The knife parted the ropes without so much as a sawing motion, wickedly sharp. Hack leaned close, his breath hot and smelling of a spittoon. "You try anything and you'll be sorry. I won't kill you. I'll kill one of them kids." He ran his thumb along the blade then returned the knife to its sheath.

He tugged Lily to her feet. Brady shoved Rose back at her and drew his gun. The baby had stopped crying and now hic-cupped and chuffed, rubbing her eyes with her dirty little fists. Lily wrapped her arms around the baby and stepped around a stream of water pouring through the rafters.

"To the wagon, if you please?" Though Brady phrased it as a question, his stony stare made it an order, as did a flick of his wrist, motioning with the gun toward the door.

She hurried to do his bidding, the death of Wanda all too fresh in her mind. As she stepped outside, she tried to shelter Rose's bare head from the rain.

A high, rickety-looking wagon on spindly wheels sat in front of the cabin, two raw-boned dark horses harnessed to it. The children, arms wrapped around their up-drawn knees, sat in the back, ducking their heads and trying to be small. As painful as it was to hand Rose over, Lily had no choice when Brady jabbed the gun into Lily's ribs. She passed the baby to the older girl, a lump in her throat the size of a peach. Brady rum-maged under the front seat and dragged out a dirty folded tarpaulin. He tossed it to the boy. "Cover up. And you" — he jerked his head toward Lily — "get up there and drive."

Hack swung aboard his mount, a shaggy

pinto with a malevolent, white-ringed eye. The animal shook his head and stretched out his neck, baring huge yellow teeth, as nasty as his master.

Lily clambered onto the seat and bent to pick up the moisture-slick lines, blinking as the wind whipped the rain into her eyes. She put her foot on the brake and braced herself.

Brady seated himself next to her and pressed the barrel of his handgun into her side. "Hack, I'll take the road up past the Dandy Dust Mine then head back south. I'll check in with the boss. I'll have some tall explaining to do, no doubt." He nudged her to release the brake.

A cannonball of fear grew in Lily's middle as she contemplated what would happen to her and the children when they met Brady's boss. Brady was bad enough. How much worse must the man who hired him be? She glanced over her shoulder to the canvas-covered humps in the back.

Lightning split the sky, followed hard by a booming roll of thunder. Hack's horse sidled, throwing its head up. Hack had to shout over the storm. "I doubt the boss will be in any mood to hear your fancy talking. First his rustling operation on the Cross B goes south. Now the money from his kidnapping scheme is drying up. You'll be lucky if he doesn't kill you. I've had it with this baby-snatching lark. I'll do my best to waylay those two fellows on your trail, but after that, I'm going back to robbing stages."

Lily's heart raced at the thought of Hack lying in wait for Trace and Cal. How could she help them? How could she warn them? Clutching the reins, she scanned the tree line. Her wet dress clung to her and sent chills across her skin. The wind lashed the tops of the pines. Her teeth began to chatter, and she clamped them shut. From the back, one of the children cried softly. She wished she could gather them tight and give them reassurances, but what could she say?

Brady didn't spare them a glance, keeping his eyes on Hack. "Anything you want me to tell the boss when I see him?"

"Tell him I'll meet up with him in a couple of weeks at the usual place. Give him some time to cool off. He's going to be spitting railroad spikes when he finds out how you loused things up. If he wasn't under the weather right now, I wouldn't give much for your chances, especially once he learns he's back to purloining stage passengers' pocket watches. He might have to start robbing banks."

Brady shook his head. "I'll be back up and

running in no time. I just need a couple of good men."

Hack spit, adjusted his hat to shield his face, and kicked his mount. His voice drifted over his shoulder as his horse pounded toward the trees. "Watch your back."

Brady poked Lily with his gun, and she slapped the reins wetly against the team's rumps. The wagon lurched, and Lily's mind raced. Brady pointed to the right, and she brought the horses' heads around. They were heading away from the cabin, away from town and the direction from which she'd come.

How far back was Trace? Had he found her message in the hotel room? Had he found the ribbon on the path? And if he hadn't, how was she going to protect these precious children?

A slight movement on the edge of the clearing caught her eye.

EIGHTEEN

By his best guess, they were only a few hundred yards from where Tilda had said the cabin was when it began to rain. Trace stopped and untied his slicker from behind his saddle and shrugged into it. A rivulet of water streamed from a branch over his head and spattered off his hat brim.

Miserable weather. He hated getting wet. And Lily must be soaked by now, if she wasn't under cover. Fool woman, traipsing around in a storm. With every step along the trail, he hoped to find her, but the farther they went, the less hope he had that she'd escaped the clutches of Brady and company. They pressed on.

The trees thinned ahead, and Trace stopped on the edge of the clearing. As promised, a ramshackle cabin stood rotting in the center of the open space. He watched it for a moment, coming to terms with the fact that Lily had to have gotten this far and he hadn't caught up with her before she did. "Let's get off this trail." If Brady decided to head into town, they'd come right by here. Better to hide the horses and get the lay of the land. He wove through the brush and tree trunks until they were well away from the path. He tethered his horse and motioned for Cal to do the same.

"The saloon girl was right." Cal tipped his head forward, and rain ran off his hat brim in a waterfall. "What do you want to do?"

Trace slid his rifle from his scabbard and lifted the collar of his slicker to keep the water from running down his neck. With a slow, quiet motion, he cocked the rifle and jacked a shell into the chamber. He took a moment to make sure his emotions were under control, jailing his feelings in the back of his mind and letting his instincts as a lawman take over once more. "Let's get a little closer. See who's home. Keep your eyes peeled for Lily. She might be in the trees, or they might have her by now."

Thunder rumbled overhead, echoing the rumbling around his heart. Thinking of Lily made it hard to keep his feelings locked in their cell. If Brady caught her snooping around, chances were excellent he'd kill her on the spot. Wet as he was, Trace's mouth went dustpan-dry at the thought.

Cal followed on his heels as he circled the clearing, keeping to the woods until they faced the cabin doorway. About forty yards of open ground, Trace surmised. Could he make it across the open space and crouch under that window without being seen? He had only taken two steps when he froze and ducked down and back into the bushes.

The rattle of a wagon drifted toward them through the rain. A scream and a gunshot rent the air.

Lily! Trace jumped up, but Cal's arm snagged him and jerked him back into the scrub. Cal dropped down beside him as a team and wagon emerged from the trees behind the shack and stopped in front of the door.

"Let me go." Trace shrugged, but his brother's grip refused to loosen.

"No."

His whisper screamed in his head. "But that was Lily's voice!"

"There's nothing you can do right now. Use your head." Cal shook Trace's arm, his expression fierce. "I know you want to rush the place, but you'll spook them into shooting those kids."

The driver — the knife-sharpening kidnapper from the hotel room — hopped down and went inside.

Trace strained to hear something — anything — that would tell him what was going on in the cabin.

After what seemed an age, the kidnapper emerged with a child under each arm. Casually, like throwing feed bags, he tossed them into the wagon. "Stay put or I'll gut you like a hog at butchering time." Thanks to the pouring rain, he had to raise his voice, and Trace was able to hear every word. The children got his message as well, for they scooted close together and put their faces on their knees.

Trace's hands tightened on his rifle. He could drill the man right now, easy as a spring breeze, but as Cal said, that might panic Brady — if he was in the cabin like their saloon girl informant had said — into doing something foolish. Better to wait and see what they were planning. He'd much rather have them all in the open than holed up in the cabin. And there might be more than just the two men to consider as well. Someone had to have been watching the rest of these kids while Brady was in Jardin.

As if the thought conjured him up, Brady emerged toting a kid, his spare, pale frame unmistakable even in the teeth of a storm. He wore no hat, and rain plastered his white-blond hair to his head. He lifted the

224

child into the wagon with more care than the other man had shown. Trace crouched perfectly still as Brady's light eyes swept his way.

The smaller man — Hack, Tilda had called him — reemerged, this time with Lily, who was holding an infant.

Relief at seeing Lily alive made Trace dizzy.

Cal put his hand on Trace's arm, and Trace realized he'd raised his rifle and trained it on Hack. "Easy there, big brother."

Trace lowered his gun. Cal was right. They had to take this slow. There might be more in the cabin.

Lily looked unharmed, at least as far as Trace could tell. Relief faded to anger. He had known she'd get into trouble. Now he had to rescue her along with the children. Once more he set his feelings aside and focused on the job ahead. Time enough when everyone was safe to light into her for being so foolhardy. He strained to hear through the patter of rain.

Brady had his gun out and pointed at Lily. He motioned her into the driver's seat, then climbed aboard the wagon and tossed a tarp back toward the children. His voice carried across the clearing. "Hack, I'll take the road up past the Dandy Dust Mine then head back south. I'll check in with the boss. I'll have some tall explaining to do, no doubt."

The Dandy Dust Mine? Trace glanced at Cal, who shrugged. So Brady wasn't the boss. Trace concentrated on Hack's reply. "I doubt the boss will be in any mood to hear your fancy talking. First his rustling operation on the Cross B goes south. Now the money from his kidnapping scheme is drying up. You'll be lucky if he doesn't kill you. I've had it with this baby-snatching lark. I'll do my best to waylay those two fellows on your trail, but after that, I'm going back to robbing stages."

Cal nudged Trace's elbow, but Trace only nodded, keeping his focus on the men. So whoever this boss was, he had planned the rustling that had devastated the Cross B ranch this past spring. Alec, foreman of the Cross B and married to the owner's daughter, Clara, would be interested in that little tidbit.

Lily picked up the lines and released the brake. Rain soaked her dress and hair.

Frustration at not being able to help her right then gnawed at Trace.

Cal inched closer, his normally easygoing expression grim. "What do you want to do? We can take them both down right now."

Trace shook his head. "He's got a gun on Lily. Can't risk it." Though Trace could ventilate Brady's head with one shot at this range, there was every chance Brady would jerk that trigger and shoot Lily.

"You want me to follow Hack?" Cal's bright blue eyes trained on the pinto disappearing down the trail they'd come up.

Trace was torn. He needed Cal to help him rescue Lily and the kids, but he didn't want Hack to get away. For once, his lawman's instincts were frozen.

Lily slapped the reins and turned the horses around.

Trace leaned forward, willing her not to do anything stupid before he found some way to take Brady down.

Trace made his decision. "Go after Hack. Watch your back, and don't let him get the drop on you."

NINETEEN

Lily leaned away from the barrel of the gun and swiped her hand across her wet face. Water dripped from her chin. She'd lost track of what was tears and what was rain. Had her mind played tricks on her, making her think she'd spied a cowboy hat in the trees along the clearing? Or had Trace actually found her? "What are you going to do with us?" She voiced the question screaming in her head.

"Just drive." Brady sat as if on a pleasant outing. "We're not far."

Not far from where? Trees blocked her view on all sides and even overhead. The wagon jounced and rocked over the rutted, muddy track littered with stones and forest debris. She braced her feet on the footrest and tried to look like she was urging the team on, while hoping and praying she was going slow enough to give Trace time to catch up. As often as she dared, she checked over her shoulder on the children and looked for anyone following them.

"You can stop that. No one will come rescue you. Hack will ambush those two clodhoppers you were with. Nobody gets past Hack. He's dry-gulched more than his fair share of men before. Two more won't bother him." Brady's matter-of-fact tone, calmly discussing the demise of her husband and brother-in-law, made her blood boil.

"They aren't clodhoppers. They're working for a United States Marshal, and they're more than a match for you and Hack and a dozen others." She wanted to shock him, to make him afraid, but the piercing stare he turned on her made her regret her rash words.

"Is that so?" His calculating tone chilled her more than the rain.

Trace was right. She talked too much.

He said no more for a while as the wagon lurched along, but he made sure his gun stayed pressed into her ribs.

She had trouble navigating a rather sharp turn in the track, and the wagon bucked over a boulder and clattered back to the soggy ground.

Brady shoved her with his arm. "Stop here."

Lily looked around her. A small track led

off to the right, too narrow for a wagon. "Why? What's here?" She didn't pull up the horses, and they plodded on a few more steps. Stopping could mean nothing good for her and the children. She had to keep them in the wagon and dragging up this muddy slope to give Trace time to catch up to them. "What are you going to do to us?"

Brady didn't answer her question, just turned on his seat and cocked the pistol, aiming it at the canvas in the wagon bed. He raised one white eyebrow at her.

Her throat tightened and her heart pitched. She yanked on the reins. "Don't. I've stopped." Her lungs worked like a blacksmith's bellows, but she couldn't seem to draw a decent breath until he lowered his gun.

He showed no triumph over forcing her to do his will. Did he feel nothing? He was a walking corpse, dead inside, and well beyond reasoning with. "Get the children."

Lily climbed down, grasping the side of the wagon when her feet slipped on the dead leaves and mud. She knocked her knee against the wheel, and tears smarted in her nose and eyes. A throbbing ache started in her leg, but she forced herself upright and limped to the tailgate. She brushed against a bush and received a cascade of droplets in response. Her cold hands shook as she lifted the canvas.

Four pairs of round eyes stared back at her, hopeful yet wary. "Where are we?" The boy shrugged the tarp off and looked around.

"I don't know. Help me get the kids down. And keep quiet. Don't twist his tail." She motioned toward Brady, who stood off to the side, staring down the trail they'd ascended.

His crossed arms supported his gun, which he had trained in their direction. As she drew each child toward the end of the tailgate, Brady stepped forward and cut the ropes binding their ankles. He left their hands tied.

Lily took Rose, and the three other children edged out of the wagon and crowded close, holding her skirts and shivering.

Brady pointed to the side trail. "Get moving."

Lily put Rose on her hip and directed the others to go ahead of her. Rocks and roots littered the uneven uphill trail, and branches, heavy with water, hung over the way, soaking her with each step. She trod hard, trying to leave deep footprints, praying with every step that Trace wasn't far behind.

Trace pointed his horse toward the gap in the trees behind the cabin where the wagon had disappeared. The trail, a rocky, rutted upslope strewn with pine straw and dead leaves, showed the wheel tracks plainly in the mud. His horse plunged up the slope, hooves clacking off rocks and roots.

Trace grabbed hold of his anger once more and slowed his horse. All the racket he was making, he might as well blow a bugle and let Brady know he was coming. The wind stirred the treetops, and — he hoped — masked some of the sounds of his approach.

How far would Brady go? Who was this boss he was going to meet? And what were his plans for Lily and the kids? His thoughts went to Cal. Had he caught up with Hack? Or had Hack caught up with Cal? Trace hated that they'd had to split up, and unlike himself, he wavered on his decision a dozen times.

The trail bent sharply to the right, and when Trace rounded the corner, he yanked back on the reins, ducking his horse into the undergrowth and slipping from the saddle. He'd nearly collided with the back of the wagon. He used his rifle to lower a branch blocking his view.

The empty wagon. The horses stood abandoned, heads down, lines slack. With cautious steps, he approached and lifted one corner of the canvas hanging off the back of the wagon. He didn't know whether to be relieved or disappointed when he found nothing underneath.

Footprints littered the ground, being slowly dissolved by the rain, though the showers had slacked off a bit. The trail led off to the right and into the trees.

Trace stepped off the path and slipped through the trees parallel to the track, hoping to come abreast of them while remaining unseen.

Rose's weight dragged at Lily, and her wet and muddy skirts caught on every branch and bush along the trail. Her throbbing knee protested every step, making her limp and lurch and becoming stiffer as they clambered up the grade.

Brady prodded them all on with his ever-present Colt and his cold, unflinching stare. Whenever their pace lagged, he would give one of them a shove.

She lost count of the number of times one of them fell into the muck, the bound hands of the children making it hard for them to keep their balance. The boy, his face scratched and bleeding, turned a woeful face up to Lily, but she could do nothing to help him.

"How much farther?" Surely Trace had caught up to them by now. Why didn't he help her? What was he waiting for? Was he even back there at all? *Lord, I can't do this.*

"Not far."

"Why are you doing this? Why don't you just let us go?" *Help me. Show me what to do.*

"Be quiet."

Lily stopped when the trees thinned on what had once been a cleared space on the side of the hill. She stood with most of her weight on one leg, panting, leaning against a tree. With one arm holding Rose, she reached down with the other to massage her knee.

The forest had begun to reclaim the cleared area, with shoulder-high saplings and scrub encroaching. A massive derrick stood like a giant tripod in the center, and a slag heap overgrown with weeds and seedlings hulked off to the side. Broken shacks and dilapidated crates and barrels moldered in the drizzle. Lighting flashed, thunder boomed, and the rain increased once more.

Water poured down the hillside, cascading and melding into newborn rivers that raced to join others.

"What is this place?" Lily shifted Rose to her other hip and picked a wet leaf off the baby's hair. The infant's lips were bluish, and her cheeks pale. She blinked and ducked her head onto Lily's shoulder. Lily wrapped her tight and tried to warm her, knowing it was ridiculous in this deluge but not knowing what else to do. There wasn't a dry spot in sight.

"Never mind. Get moving." Brady pushed her toward the derrick.

A metal cage hung from the boom arm by a rust-furred chain. Once used to transport men and ore, it now rocked gently over the vertical shaft. A waterfall spilled over the side of the hole and disappeared into the darkness below.

With sickening awareness, Lily knew Brady planned to force her and the children into that cage. He'd send them to the bottom of the Dandy Dust Mine, and no one would ever find them. If the fall didn't kill them, they'd drown. Her arms tightened around Rose so hard the baby cried out.

Lily whirled to face Brady. "Don't do this. This is monstrous. This is murder." She didn't know why she tried to reason with him. He'd already proven that killing meant nothing to him.

"Get over there and quit babbling. I've told you I can't abide a blathering woman." He flicked his wrist. "I've got to move quickly, and I can't be hampered by you. Now that I know there are marshals on my trail, it's time to jettison the deadweight." He stalked to the winch and inspected it. "Ah, here we are." He hefted a hammer. "One blow to this pin and the winch releases. A quick drop and a sudden stop."

Lily scanned the area, looking for some way of escape. She had to distract him, delay him somehow so help could come. She bent low and whispered to the children crouched at her knees. "Don't let him put you in that lift. When I give you the signal, you've got to run. Scatter like quail, all right? You've got to hide in the bushes. Help's coming, but we've got to stall. Understand?"

Three pairs of eyes stared back. The boy's sparked with hope — a hope Lily prayed was justified — and nodded.

"Take Rose." She handed the baby to the older girl. "I'll keep Brady busy, but you've got to run. Run and hide." How she would keep Brady busy was anybody's guess, but she had to try. "Please, Lord, protect us.

Help us, and send Trace to us soon." She whispered the prayer into the top of Rose's head.

"Whatever you're planning, stop it. It won't work." Brady ignored the water streaming down his long face. "Time to go."

She waited until he came close to her. "Now! Run!" Lily screamed, and the children scampered toward the undergrowth, each taking a different route. She whirled, her twisted knee buckling, doubled up her fist, and punched Brady as hard as she could in the middle.

Brady's air rushed out, and he made a wild grab for her. "You — !"

She staggered backward, stumbling and flailing to keep her feet. Out of the corner of her eye, she saw the girl disappear into the bushes with Rose. At least Lily had accomplished that much.

Brady's arm came up holding the revolver.

Lily closed her eyes and turned her back, not wanting to see her own murder.

Trace's hands shook. What was she doing, provoking Brady that way? Did she want to get shot? He slipped behind a tree and positioned his rifle in the fork of two branches. A hundred yards, uphill, in a driving rain. He called upon every ounce of his skill as a marksman, knowing if he missed it would cost him Lily's life.

His shot coincided with Brady's, and his heart leapt into his throat when Lily fell. He'd been too late.

TWENTY

Trace yanked his rifle out of the fork of the tree and started up the slope to where Brady lay. He couldn't see Lily from his position, but she had to be close by.

Why? Why had she provoked Brady that way? He kept his rifle pointed at the sprawled man, though he knew he'd hit him dead center.

"Lily!" His voice was lost in a crash of thunder and he had to yell again. His throat felt like someone had stuffed it with an old sock.

His lawman's eye swept over Brady, all the while searching the tall grass for Lily. One shot, right through the temple. Brady had fallen instantly, his gun a few inches from his limp hand. Trace took the precaution of picking up the firearm and stuffing it into his belt, though he knew Brady would never fire it again.

A baby's cry filtered through the trees.

Rose. He nearly leapt in the air when a small hand touched his.

Trying to calm his ricocheting heart, he looked down at a girl of about six. Her wet hair hung like rats' tails over her face, and her dress — hard to tell the color with all the mud — hugged her body in dripping folds. Her woebegone little face made something in his chest twist up and ache. She said nothing but tucked her little hand into his and clung to him. Her lower lip shook, and he realized her teeth were chattering. He scooped her up and headed into the tall grass.

Then he saw her. "Lily!"

His heart, which had pounded hard in his chest since the moment he realized she had left the hotel room, now stopped beating altogether. She lay facedown, a good thirty feet down the slope from where Brady had come to a rest, near the base of a small pine tree. Its lower branches covered her legs. She wasn't moving. Rain splattered down on her limp form.

Trace let the little girl slide from his arms. "Wait here."

A rock of emotion lodged somewhere just behind his Adam's apple and stayed there as he skidded down the slope toward her. Fearing the worst, he squatted beside her.

Lily's dress had soaked up a bushel of mud, obscuring the flower pattern into a yellowish-brown paste. He ran his hand over her back, searching for a bullet wound. When his hand encountered the rise and fall caused by her breathing, he let out his own breath. She was still alive. As gently as he could, he turned her and gathered her into his arms.

Moisture had gathered her lashes into spiky points. A smear of mud followed the curve of her cheek, and pine needles clung to her hair. Her skin was cold.

A thin boy slipped between clumps of grass and stopped. "You here to help us?"

Trace nodded, feeling for broken bones.

"Is she dead? Wanda's dead. Did Brady shoot her like he shot Wanda?"

Trace shook his head, pushing the hair off Lily's forehead. A nasty swelling pushed out from her temple. He checked her again for signs of a gunshot wound, and when he found none, he started breathing again.

The other girl he'd seen stepped close, holding a baby.

Lily stirred in Trace's arms.

Thankfulness rushed through him. "Lily?"

Her eyelids fluttered and her lips parted. She groaned and opened her eyes, blinking and trying to focus. She stiffened. "Trace?"

Seeing her beautiful turquoise eyes, knowing she hadn't been shot, both relieved and angered him. He wanted to shake her until her teeth rattled for scaring him like that, for leaving the hotel room, for putting herself in danger. He clamped his lips tight. He had to maintain his control.

She relaxed. "Is Rose all right? Are the rest of the children?"

"Fine." He forced the word out through his clenched teeth.

"Brady?"

"Dead."

Lily's head ached and her knee throbbed. Trace deposited her in the closest shack and left to get his horse. The children huddled around her, wrapped in Trace's slicker. So far, she'd only been able to get one-word answers out of Trace, but her head hurt too much to worry about it. They were safe. That was all that mattered.

It took three trips to get them all down to the wagon. The last trip Trace made down with Brady's body tied over his saddle. Trace tethered the horse to the tailgate.

With quick jerks, he loosened his bedroll from behind his saddle and shook out the blanket and ground sheet. Without a word he took his slicker off the kids, bundled them into the blanket, and covered them with the ground sheet in the back of the wagon. He used the filthy canvas from the wagon to cover Brady's body. "Here." He held out the slicker so Lily could slip her arms into it.

She slid into it gratefully and picked up Rose, tucking her inside the big garment. Lily shook her head when he tried to lift her into the wagon bed beside the children. "I'll ride on the seat with you."

"Fine."

Again the terse comment. He'd never been exactly verbose, but this was beyond taciturn. The kisses and embraces she'd anticipated upon their reunion dissipated like mist in the desert. "Are you all right?"

"Fine." He placed Lily on the wagon seat and went to the horses' heads to help turn them on the narrow track.

"Where's Cal?"

"Garnett."

"Trace, what's wrong? Aren't you glad to see me?"

He didn't answer for a long time.

"Well?"

"Yep." He sounded like he was choking on a dry biscuit. He didn't look at her, just mounted the wagon and clucked to the team.

She gave up. If he wouldn't talk, he wouldn't talk. Maybe he was keyed up from the fight. After all, he'd just shot and killed a man. Or perhaps he was just reticent in front of the children. They'd sort it out later. She contented herself with cuddling Rose inside the roomy slicker.

The rain had let up again, though under the dripping trees it hardly felt like it. Trace, in shirtsleeves, had to be feeling the chill, but from the forbidding expression on his face, she decided not to comment.

The children crowded around her when they stopped in the clearing to retrieve Wanda's body. Lily wanted to hug them all and to cleanse from their minds the horror they'd faced, but no words would erase what they'd seen. She prayed time would dull the edges.

Dark fell before they made it back to Garnett.

Cal met them at the livery, his face a thundercloud in the lantern light. "I lost Hack. I'm sorry, Trace. I was hot on his trail when a big crack of lighting struck a tree nearby. My horse spooked and pitched me. Took me awhile to chase him down, and by that time Hack had disappeared. I've been all over town looking for him, but if he came back to Garnett, he's gone now." He scowled.

"Forget it. Help me get them to the hotel." Trace didn't even look at her or the children when he spoke. A snowdrift had more warmth.

When Lily was rested up, she was going to lambaste him. How dare he treat them so coldly? They'd been through a miserable time, but he was acting as if it were all her fault. Where had the soft caresses, the kisses, the hope for their future gone? He was back to being a surly bear, snarling at people.

Cal smiled at Lily, his expression softening. "Glad to see you're all right. Don't know what Trace would've done if something would've happened to you."

Probably danced a jig the way he was acting. Her eyelids drooped. She was so tired she thought she might sleep for a week.

Their room was still available at the hotel. Cal rousted the clerk and had water and a tub hauled upstairs.

Trace disappeared, returning after a while with some clean clothing. "Here. The best I could do this time of night."

"Thank you." Lily looked down at her dress. The mud had dried, stiffening the skirts until they crackled; small pieces of dirt crumbled off each time she knelt to wash a child.

She stumbled when she stood away from the tub, her sore knee giving out on her. Trace caught her in his arms. She smiled up at him, anticipating a kiss or at least a shared moment, but his face was like a mask, and he set her away from him.

Confused and hurt, she began dressing the now-clean children.

Cal raided the hotel kitchen. Though everyone was hungry, they were all so tired they could barely eat.

Lily tucked the kids in, the girls and Rose in the bed and the boy on Trace's bedroll on the floor. They fell asleep before she turned down the lamp.

Cal entered with two more buckets of hot water.

Trace hadn't returned after dropping off the clothing.

Lily hugged her arms across her middle. "Cal, what's wrong with Trace? Why's he so mad? And where did he go?"

He looked up from refilling the tub. Shrugging, he angled the dressing screen to give her some privacy and winked at her. "Don't worry about Trace. He's chewing on something, and he'll spit it out eventually. You scared him bad when you weren't here. It'll take him a little time to sort things out in his head. He's gone to see about getting

Brady and the woman buried. You look like you're about to drop. Get cleaned up and don't worry. Trace and I will take turns standing guard. I'll be in the hall. Knock when you're done."

Lily shrugged, too tired to care much at the moment what her husband's problem was. The bath relaxed her further. Her knee, which she'd thought was just bruised, bore a nasty cut that had bled and scabbed over. It hurt more now that she knew how bad it was, which was silly, but she couldn't help it.

The dress Trace had brought her was at least two sizes too big. She slipped into it, grateful to be clean at last, and threw everyone's dirty clothes into the bathwater to soak overnight. Hair wrapped in a towel, she slid into bed beside Rose, and just before her eyes closed, she remembered she'd forgotten to knock to let Cal know she was finished.

Twenty-One

Trace spent the night in the rocker in the hotel room, dozing and waking by turns to stare at his sleeping wife and wonder where to go from here. Anger and hurt burned through him, and yet, while she slept the sleep of exhaustion, he wanted nothing more than to hold her tight and make her promise never to lie to him again.

He shook his head. What good would her promises do? She'd promised before and lied. His guts knotted. How had he been so stupid as to let her into his heart? Well, no more. He'd keep her at arm's length.

They traveled to Jardin in the wagon the next day. The three older children, fed, clean, and away from Brady and Wanda, revived like flowers in a spring rain. Though they stayed close to Lily, Trace felt sure they would be all right when they got back to their families. Pastor Greeley and Mei Lin welcomed them into their house and agreed to care for the children, including the Indian baby they'd rescued earlier, until Maxwell could reunite them with their parents.

Trace questioned Bobcat, looking for leads to Brady's and Hack's boss, but Bobcat had no information. By focusing on the case, Trace was able to avoid Lily and her questioning eyes. She tried twice to draw him out, but he rebuffed her. After that, she quit trying.

She and Mei Lin talked as if they were old friends while looking after the children. In spite of all she'd been through, Lily managed to bake a pie for dessert that night. Trace wasn't sure who enjoyed it more, Cal or the kids. Though he had long enjoyed Lily's baking skills, because of the distance between them, the pie tasted of damp newspaper to Trace.

Cal saw them onto the stage with Rose in the morning; then he took off for Money Creek riding his own horse and leading Trace's.

Trace and Lily had the coach to themselves, and for the first time since he'd met her, Lily remained silent. The chatter he'd become accustomed to had dried up. She held the baby on her lap and stared out the window. And for the first time, he couldn't tell what she was thinking.

The baby, on the other hand, never stopped jabbering. In the early morning light, Trace got his first good look at Rose. She was bald as a cue ball and drooling like a lead steer, but in spite of that, her eyes caught Trace's attention. Pure turquoise, just like Lily's. She grinned at him, two perfect white teeth showing in her bottom gum. He put his hand out, and she grabbed his finger. He marveled at her little hand, and when she leaned forward, it seemed natural to reach for her.

Lily let her go into his arms.

Rose weighed next to nothing. She seemed fascinated by his mustache, reaching out with a splayed hand and stroking it. He wiggled his upper lip, and Rose giggled. Then her gaze fell on the star pinned on his vest. She squealed and tugged on it. He slipped it off and handed it to her after making sure the pin was secure. He turned her on his lap to face Lily, and she leaned back against him and gnawed on the star, her little hands wrapped around two of the points.

The realization that Rose was now, in fact, his daughter swept over him. He turned the idea over in his mind and found he didn't entirely dislike it. A daughter. And a wife. A wife he was in love with.

"Lily, I think it's time you and I had a talk."

She turned her beautiful eyes toward him. "Really?" Her voice was colder than the wind off the mountains.

"Um, yes."

"Well, I don't." She crossed her arms and closed her eyes.

Trace blinked.

The horses began to slow. They'd arrived in Money Creek.

Lily took Rose from Trace the minute the stage stopped. The big idiot. She allowed him to help her from the stage, but as soon as her feet hit the ground, she limped away.

Georgia stepped onto the porch of the Rusty Bucket, and when she saw Lily, she let out a yell. Lily found herself and Rose squashed against Georgia's considerable bosom. "Oh, girl, you found our precious baby." Georgia made several snorting noises that sounded like she might be stifling tears.

Lily allowed herself to be comforted, something she'd been longing for from Trace but hadn't gotten. The big idiot.

"Lily."

She disengaged herself from Georgia and handed her the baby before she turned to confront her husband. "What?"

"We need to talk."

"Talk? What for?"

"Well, we are married. I'd say we have some things to talk about."

Georgia gasped behind Lily. "Married?"

Lily was conscious of the many eyes and ears around them, but she didn't care. She stalked to the edge of the boardwalk and poked Trace in the chest. "For days you've told me to keep my mouth shut. And ever since you shot Brady, you've been treating me like a criminal. I don't want to talk to you. I can't trust you anymore." Having him so close, looking into his gray eyes, Lily wanted to throw herself into his arms and cry, demanding that he fix her broken heart. Right after she slugged him for being such an idiot.

Trace's eyes widened. "*You* can't trust *me?* I'm not the one who lied and ran off the minute your back was turned."

She blinked. "I never lied." Her hands fisted on her hips. "When did I ever lie to you?"

"When you promised to stay in the hotel room." He stepped close until they stood nose to nose. "I don't know how you found out about the cabin where Rose was being held, but you should've waited for me to get back before scooting off to confront Brady."

"But I had no choice! When I got Hack's note, I had to go. I wanted to stay, believe me."

"What note?" He went still, his eyes boring into hers.

"The note that said I had to meet him within the half hour or he'd kill Rose. The note he made me return to him so you wouldn't know where I went." Her throat burned and her stomach clenched as she remembered how scared she'd been. "I was frantic. If I stayed, she'd be killed. I tried to think through what you would do, and I knew there was no way you'd stay in that hotel room. And besides" — she poked him again — "I knew you'd come after me. I left you the message, and I left the ribbon on the path." A stray thought flitted through her head. "Why do you have that ribbon anyway? You did find it again, right?"

"The ribbon was my mama's, and yes, I found it again." He stroked his mustache. "It's the same color as your eyes." He cocked his head and scrunched his eyes closed for a moment. "Wait a minute. You left the hotel room because you *knew* I'd come after you?"

"Of course. You're a lawman, and you're

my husband. I trusted you. You knew I needed you, and you came."

He paused for a moment, considering her words. "Do you know what I went through when I found you were gone?" His expression softened as he spoke, and his eyes took on a warm, questioning look. Gently, he cupped her shoulders. "I thought you didn't trust any man."

"I didn't trust just any man." Tears thickened her voice. "I trusted *you.*" The broken places in her heart began to heal as she voiced the words.

"You took an awful risk."

She nodded, blinking back tears. "Trusting someone . . . *loving* someone is an awful risk, I've found."

He lifted his hands to caress her cheeks. "Lily McConnell . . ."

She shivered at the sound of her married name on his lips.

"I love you."

She wound her arms around his neck. "Trace McConnell, I love you, too."

He wrapped her in his arms and lifted her off the porch, holding her against him with her feet off the ground. His mustache brushed her cheek, and his lips covered hers in a kiss that spoke of forgiveness for the past and promises of the future.

EPILOGUE

Lily looked up when the bell over the door jangled, though from Rose's squeal she knew who had walked in. Only one man elicited that response from her daughter.

"Dadadadada." The baby's pudgy hands beat the tabletop where Lily had pulled her high chair close. She strained against the tea towel tied around her waist to hold her in.

Trace strode across the bakery, his mustache twitching. "How're my best girls?"

Warm tickles spread through Lily. Even after two months of marriage, she couldn't believe he was really hers. She swiped at a couple of stray hairs tickling her cheek then went back to rolling out piecrusts. "Better once I get these into the oven." Six pie tins waited on the counter to be filled. "Georgia's orders keep me hopping." And she was grateful for the patronage. Their financial situation was by no means secure, what with the mortgage and a growing baby to care for. Trace's salary as town sheriff and her earnings from the bakery had to stretch, but thankfully, God continued to provide for their needs.

He squatted to investigate why he couldn't lift Rose from her chair. "She lassoed you, punkin, didn't she?"

Rose drummed her heels and slapped the table again with a happy crow.

How Lily loved to see them together. Trace was a wonderful father. "I had to rope her in. She's climbing like a squirrel."

Rose's string of spools clacked to the floor.

Trace unknotted the towel and lifted the baby.

Lily transferred dough to a pie plate. "What brings you here in the middle of the morning?"

He shrugged and looked away. "Powers came back to work today. He's all healed up, so he doesn't need me anymore."

Her hands stilled. "Not even as a deputy?"

"He says not."

Poor Trace. The mortgage sat heavy on him, she knew, and now to be out of work. All he wanted was to be a lawman. She wiped her hands on her apron and rounded the tin-topped worktable to wrap her arms around his waist and lean into his side.

"We'll make out."

He kissed the top of her head. "Sure we will. As you're always telling me, the Lord won't forsake us."

She stared up into his gray eyes.

He rubbed his thumb between her eyebrows. "You always get a crease right here when you're worrying. You aren't thinking I'll up and run, are you?" His voice teased, but his eyes bored into hers.

"Not a chance, mister." She smiled and hugged him tight. "You'd never leave us."

"That's right. I'm not going anywhere."

The bell jangled again and Cal entered, smiling and sniffing the air like a dog. "You wouldn't happen to have any pecan, would you?"

Lily slipped from Trace's arms and went to the pie safe. "I'll get you a slice." Next to Georgia, Cal was Lily's best and most frequent customer. She slid a generous portion onto a plate and snagged a fork from the jar on the counter. "This one's on the house."

He spun the plate around and started at the crust side, like always. "You're a blessed man, Trace McConnell." Cal closed his eyes and savored the first bite.

Trace put his arm around Lily's shoulders and squeezed. "That I know, little brother."

Two more bites and then Cal dug in his pocket. "This pie's so good I almost forgot why I came over here." He slid a packet out and dropped it with a *clunk* on the counter. "Maxwell's in town. He sent this over."

Lily poured Cal a cup of coffee while Trace opened the envelope. He went so still, Lily's heart began bumping painfully against her ribs.

Trace glanced at Cal. "You know what's in here?"

Cal grinned and nodded, lifting the coffee cup to his lips. "Maxwell told me."

"What is it?" Lily wanted to snatch the pages out of Trace's hand.

He looked up, gray eyes shining, and his mustache twitched. "Take a look." He twisted his palm around to display a silver badge, holding it out toward her. "My appointment came through. I'm a U.S. Marshal."

"Maxwell said he'd see you later today to take the oath. And he wants to talk to both of us about the stage robberies." Cal scraped the plate with his fork to get the last few crumbs. "Still the best pie ever, Lily."

She nodded, trying to take in Trace's words. A U.S. marshal — the job he'd wanted since he was a little boy. She fingered the badge, tears smarting in her eyes.

"And that's not all." Trace flipped another page to display a wanted poster. A sketch of Brady stared back at her. The cold, lifeless eyes made her shiver. "There's a reward for Brady."

Lily read the amount twice. "Five hundred dollars?"

"Yep." Cal drained his coffee cup. "Maxwell said he brought the money. It's at the bank waiting for you."

Overwhelmed by God's blessings, Lily sagged onto a stool. Trace put the badge in her hand, and she clutched it, the metal heavy in her palm. *Thank You, Lord.* They could pay off the mortgage and have a little left over. And Trace could be a lawman after all.

A wave of happiness broke over her. She stood and pinned the badge to Trace's vest. As she went into his arms, she realized anew how much she'd come to love and trust this man, and she tried to put every ounce of that love and trust into her kiss.

Breathless, she tucked her face into the crook of Trace's neck. His heart thumped under her ear, and he whispered, "I love you, Mrs. McConnell. For always."

ABOUT THE AUTHOR

Erica Vetsch is married to Peter and keeps the company books for the family lumber business. A homeschool mom to Heather and James, Erica loves history, romance, and storytelling. Her ideal vacation is taking her family to out-of-the-way history museums and chatting with curators about local history. She has a bachelor's degree from Calvary Bible College in secondary education: social studies. You can find her on the Web at www.onthewritepath.blogspot.com.

A NOTE FROM THE AUTHOR:

I love to hear from my readers! You may correspond with me by writing:

Erica Vetsch
Author Relations
PO Box 721
Uhrichsville, OH 44683

The employees of Thorndike Press hope you have enjoyed this Large Print book. All our Thorndike, Wheeler, and Kennebec Large Print titles are designed for easy reading, and all our books are made to last. Other Thorndike Press Large Print books are available at your library, through selected bookstores, or directly from us.

For information about titles, please call:
  (800) 223-1244

or visit our Web site at:
  http://gale.cengage.com/thorndike

To share your comments, please write:
  Publisher
  Thorndike Press
  10 Water St., Suite 310
  Waterville, ME 04901